The Little
Dark Thorn

The Little Dark Thorn

Ruth M. Arthur

illustrated by Margery Gill

Atheneum 1971 New York

Copyright © 1971 by Ruth M. Arthur
All rights reserved
Library of Congress catalog card number 74-154746
Published simultaneously in Canada by McClelland & Stewart, Ltd.
Manufactured in the United States of America
by Halliday Lithograph Corporation
West Hanover, Massachusetts
First Edition

FOR GILLIAN,
my niece and goddaughter
with love.

Author's Note

I wish to thank David Gray for his invaluable help and advice in relation to the Malayan background.

Contents

Part I
Aunt Emma's House

1

I CAN REMEMBER THE VERY FIRST TIME I CAME TO AUNT Emma's house. I was newly six years old. I stood on the doorstep trembling with cold and anxiety while my father tried the handle of the door, and finding it locked, thundered on it with the knocker.

There was a little cry from inside the house and a light rush of feet. The door was wrenched open, arms were held out, and an eager voice cried, "Oh, Robert! Is it really you? You're earlier than we expected. Come in, come in, you must be tired after such a long journey. And this is your little girl? I'm so *glad* you brought her home with you. It was the right thing to do. How are you, dearie?"

"Quite well, thank you," I answered politely, as I had been taught.

"Aunt Emma, this is Meriam. We call her Merrie," said my father.

I clutched his hand tightly and looked up into a wrinkled face and two very blue eyes. I felt clumsy and awkward in the thick clothes my father had bought for me. Also I was very tired and cross and rather frightened.

We had just arrived by air from Malaya, my father and I, and now we had come to the end of our journey—to Aunt Emma's house.

"Come along, my pet," said Aunt Emma picking me up in her arms and carrying me inside. "Your father will follow us in one minute. You're very small and light for six years old, but you're a dear little girl, aren't you?"

I didn't feel like a dear little girl at all. I only felt terribly homesick and strange, and I wanted my mother.

But I smiled so that she wouldn't know what I really felt. I didn't want her to think me impolite. My mother had taught me always to smile, even when things were very bad —it is the polite thing to do.

"Merrie is a good name for such a smiling little girl," said Aunt Emma.

My bed was beside my father's in a room at the top of many wooden steps, high above the ground and quite unlike my father's bungalow in Malaya. When I woke in the night, I had forgotten where I was, and I called softly for my mother. There were no mosquito nets—they didn't seem to need them in England. My covers had slipped off, and I was cold and began to cry.

My father tumbled out of bed and picked me up and took me in beside him and held me in his arms to warm me, but it was not enough. He was the *Tuan*, the master, it was my mother I wanted.

"Why doesn't my mother come?" I asked. "Why didn't she fly to England with us? Will she come soon? Will she come tomorrow?"

"Go to sleep, Merrie," said my father, "it is tomorrow already." He carried me back to my bed and tucked me in.

I lay in the darkness thinking about Aunt Emma's house and how quiet the night was—no gun shots, no bangs, no fires, no screams of terror in the darkness—there could not be any Communists in England. If only my mother would come, we could be happy and safe here in Aunt Emma's house. She seemed very kind, and there was someone called Cousin Jessica who walked slowly and stiffly as my mother's grandmother did when her bones were aching. Cousin Jessica was Aunt Emma's friend who lived with her. She was fat and did the cooking. The fluffy gray pussy cat belonged to her—I liked pussies.

Later, when it was light, I got up and dressed myself without waking my father. It was raining outside so I went into the kitchen where I could smell coffee. Cousin Jessica was eating at the table, and she gave me some milk and some bread and honey.

"When is my mother coming?" I asked. "Will she come soon?"

"You must ask your father, dear," said Cousin Jessica, "but I do not think she will come soon."

"Then which is the way home?" I cried desperately.

· Before she could answer, there was a bump against the door and a scratching noise. When Cousin Jessica opened it, a great woolly dog rushed into the room. He bounced up to me showing huge teeth.

I was too terrified to move. I just opened my mouth and screamed and screamed and screamed.

Aunt Emma ran in and dragged the animal away as my father rushed to me and lifted me into his arms.

"She's not used to dogs," he explained to Aunt Emma.

"But he's not a fierce dog, he only wanted to make

friends," cried Cousin Jessica.

"He's rather big, but he wouldn't bite you," Aunt Emma explained.

"Don't be frightened of him, Merrie," my father soothed me. "He's really smiling at you when he shows his teeth."

"Waterloo, you must be more gentle with the little girl," said Aunt Emma to the dog while she kept hold of his collar.

My father sat down with me on his knee, and held out his hand to the dog. "Come here, Waterloo," he said snapping his fingers. "Come and make friends with Merrie."

The big dog came quietly across the room to my father. He sat beside us, and as my father patted and talked to him, I became gradually calmer, and at last I was able to reach out my hand to pat the woolly head.

In spite of my thick dress I felt cold, and seeing this Aunt Emma lit a fire and brought a stool for me to sit close to the flames. I sat and looked at a picture book while my father and Aunt Emma talked together about Malaya, about the Communists who hid in the jungle and raided at night. I covered my ears so that I could not hear when he told her about the shooting, and the killing and the burning of the houses.

"They're very bad people, the Communists," I put in.

"How dreadful! All that violence!" exclaimed Aunt Emma. "It must have been terrifying."

"It *was*," my father replied, "though we were just on the fringe of it; other parts got it very badly."

"How thankful you must be, Robert, to have got safely home with Merrie before it spread any further."

"I feel I should have stayed out there after my job packed up, to help bring back law and order, but it was very difficult to know what to do."

"You did the right thing, Robert. You brought your little girl home to England," said Aunt Emma in a firm voice. She had no doubts about it.

Later, when the rain stopped, Aunt Emma took me in the bus down the valley to the market town.

I was still cold and I wore my thick coat. The wind howled round the trees, blowing their leaves off—such pretty leaves of gold and flame and brown.

Aunt Emma went from shop to shop, filling her basket. Then as the wind grew wilder and colder, we had some hot coffee in a shop and I warmed my icy fingers on the cup. Aunt Emma bought me a box of colored pencils and a book for drawing in, and she bought me a toy bear, a "teddy" bear she called it, with big brown ears. When we got back again to Aunt Emma's house, my mother still had not come.

Soon my father went away for a few days, and I was left with the two old women. They were kind to me. Aunt Emma took me for walks and told me stories about my father when he was a boy, and Cousin Jessica, who looked like a cozy old pussy cat, gave me nice things to eat—but they did not love me, they were just being kind. I did not belong to them.

Always, all the time, I was homesick and longing for my mother. When I asked why she did not come, no one answered me properly till I could stand it no longer. We were having breakfast when I asked once more, "Tell me, please tell me, when is my mother coming?"

The two old women looked at one another and looked away again, then Aunt Emma said, "Not just yet, dearie. Eat up your breakfast like a good girl."

"When?" I shouted exasperated. "Tell me when!"

"Ssh! Perhaps not at all, perhaps she will stay in Malaya.

You must ask your father," said Aunt Emma gruffly.

"Surely Robert must have told her," murmured Cousin Jessica, "he couldn't—"

"Nobody tells me anything!" I broke in furiously, and I picked up my plate and threw it on the floor where it smashed into pieces. My cup of milk followed it, but before I could reach anything else, Aunt Emma jumped up and seized both my hands and pulled me off my chair. So I bit her and kicked her legs as I struggled to get away.

"She's just a wild little animal!" exclaimed Cousin Jessica in a shocked voice. That maddened me more than ever. I butted and kicked and twisted about while Aunt Emma held me at arm's length. Suddenly she slapped my face, hard. With a desperate twist I wrenched myself from her grasp, ran out of the room and up the stairs. I dived under my bed and lay sobbing with rage and misery till I fell asleep.

When I awoke, I began to play with the thin gold bangle I wore with others on my wrist. It was real gold and had been my mother's, but she had given it to me just before I left for England and I wore it day and night. It felt like her touch on my wrist comforting me in this strange cold country.

I must have spent about an hour under my bed, but by the time Aunt Emma tapped on my door I was feeling quite good again.

"We'd better wash your face," Aunt Emma remarked, "and we'll have no more of those tantrums if you please, that's no way to behave. We'll say no more about it."

"I'm sorry," I said quietly and I allowed Aunt Emma to lead me by the hand to the bathroom. After all, it wasn't her fault that my mother didn't come, it was my father's; he was the one to blame, the one to question.

After a few days my father came back and told us he had got a new job in London and would only be coming to live with us at weekends. At first, I did not want him to leave me because I felt he was my only link with my mother. And that night after I was in bed, when my father came to say goodnight to me, I asked him straight out, "When is my mother coming? Why did you not bring her to England with us?"

For a moment he just stared at me without answering, then he took both my hands in his. "She is not coming here, ever," he said and his voice sounded hard, bitter. "When you are older you will understand why not. Malaya is her home, she would not be happy in England."

"I am not happy in England. Malaya is *my* home, but you brought me here!" I exclaimed indignantly.

"That's different. You are my child and half English," he said angrily. "Now listen, Merrie, you are to be a good girl and settle down here with Aunt Emma. This is your home now."

"I won't settle down!" I cried. "I hate this England! I hate you for bringing me here. You must send me back to Malaya, back to my mother. You *must!*"

"I can't do that, Merrie," he said, "it is not possible."

"Why not? *Why* not?" I demanded.

"Because your mother sent you home here with me, she begged me to take you, she wants you to grow up in England, where you are safe."

I was stunned and completely aghast. I turned on him savagely.

"It's not true! She'd never send me away from her. She can't love me any more or she'd have come with us. What will happen to her?" I asked.

"She will marry one of her own people," said my father.

"You must try to forget her, Merrie."

"I won't!" I yelled. "Go away! Go to London and never come back. I don't want you."

"Poor child, it is hard for you to understand. Some day when you are older, I'll try to explain it all to you."

He put out his hand to touch me, but I knocked it away and pushed him off my bed. He got up and left me then, and I ran into the empty room next door. I did not want to see him again, ever.

I burrowed under the covers and screwed myself up into a tight ball. My father had deceived me, cheated me when I trusted him; my mother, whom I loved best in all the world, had discarded me, abandoned me. How could she, who was gentle and sweet and loving, be so cruel.

The hurt built up inside me hard and heavy like a lump of lead. Nobody cared about me; I belonged to no one; I had no place to call my own. The whole world was against me.

"I hate them all! I'll fight them!" I sobbed into the pillow. At last my rage burned itself out, and I fell asleep exhausted.

After my father left for London the next day, Aunt Emma made me help her move all my things into the room next door.

"You can have this room to yourself, dearie," she said. I pretended I didn't care, but I was secretly very pleased.

My father's visits became fewer, sometimes only one weekend in three or four. Aunt Emma was disappointed, but she tried to make excuses for him.

"He can't come oftener," she explained, "his new work is too far away. But you are all right here with us, dearie, we will look after you."

I missed him although I would not say so; and I did not

feel all right, I felt all wrong—lost and twisted up inside and very much alone.

Aunt Emma's village was quite a small one, about twenty buildings—cottages mostly, one shop and post office, one little hotel and the mountains all round. The river flowed past one side of it, at the end of the lane where Aunt Emma's house stood, and ran parallel with the road down the valley to the lake and the market town from where the buses came. Like my grandmother's village, the *kampong* in Malaya, everyone knew everything about everyone; only here in Aunt Emma's village, there was the hotel where visitors came in the summer, strangers from the world outside. There were trees but no rubber plantations, and there were no flowers.

At the other end of the village from Aunt Emma's house lived Miss Holly, who held a class in her house in the mornings for four or five children of my age.

Aunt Emma asked me if I would like to go, too, and I said, "Why not? I'll learn to read." At first one of the other children came for me every morning and we walked along shyly together to Miss Holly's house for lessons. The other children played together and chased about till their cheeks were red, but they did not ask me to play with them. Sometimes they made fun of me because I looked different.

One day they took my teddy bear away from me and threw him into the river. I got very wet getting him out, but I managed to push two of them into the water.

Aunt Emma was angry and went to see Miss Holly. After that they left me alone, and I walked to lessons by myself.

Whenever my father came for a weekend, I scowled at him and pushed him away when he tried to pick me up in his arms; yet I was sorry when he left.

One night when I went to bed, slow feathers of white

came drifting down from the sky past my window.

"Snow, Merrie," said Aunt Emma. "Now you will see what a real English winter is like."

Next morning, the whole world was white, sparkling clear like glass in the sun, blue in the shadows.

I ran outside and plunged my hands in it. It was so cold that my hands hurt, but so beautiful that I shouted aloud. My breath hung in the air like a small cloud, and I puffed out more again and again.

"Come in at once, Merrie!" called Cousin Jessica. "You'll catch your death of cold." I did not come at once, not until I had scooped up some snow between my two hands and carried it carefully inside the house and left it in the corner by the door. I was delighted with it.

But after breakfast when I went to look, it was gone, nothing left but a puddle of water, and Cousin Jessica was cross with me for making a mess in her kitchen.

I was angry and splashed the water about the floor, making still more mess. When Cousin Jessica boxed my ears, I burst into tears and she was sorry. But I was not crying because of her, I cried because my beautiful snow was gone, and because nothing lovely ever lasted.

2

GRADUALLY, AND IN SPITE OF MY HOSTILITY, I BEGAN TO adapt myself to Aunt Emma's village. One day I realized that I had been living in Aunt Emma's house for six whole months!

Unconsciously I had been getting used to the village, to its people who knew me and spoke to me, to the children who had learned to accept me. And although I did not make a close friend of any of them, I got used to playing with them on the rocky mound that was called the village ground. Some of their games were exciting, especially the one they called the Bogey-Man game.

"What is a Bogey-Man?" I asked them.

"Giller Tyson is a Bogey-Man. He pops children into his sack and carries them away up the mountain. Look out or he'll *get* you!" they cried.

Aunt Emma allowed me to be as free as possible, to come

and go as I pleased within the village and the close-by farms, and Waterloo, who seemed to have taken me into his care, was never far away. I accepted him and although I kept my distance from him with a wary eye on his big teeth, I was quite glad of his company. The only place I was not allowed to go was across the river to the wild hill country they called the "fells," where the old quarry was. That, of course, was the very place that beckoned and lured, enticing me to enter its forbidden territory.

The first time I went across the river, I managed to escape from Waterloo while he was out on other business.

I darted along the lane and was quickly out of sight behind the hedges that bordered it. No one called me back as I had half-hoped someone would.

The lane soon became only a track and got more and more muddy with great puddles that I had to hop across. I got my boots very wet and splashed. Soon I came to the end of the track and to stepping stones across the shallows in the river—there was no bridge at this point. On the far side I could see a green path leading up over the fells to the quarry. I stood gazing at the stepping stones, but the river was full and the water was rushing over the tops of some of them. I did not dare to cross them. I decided I had better go back. But how was I to account to Cousin Jessica for the state my boots were in? It was she who cleaned them, and I did not want her asking me questions. Then I remembered Miss Holly's garden higher up the river. It was always muddy there, so I went by the back way round the village to her house. When Cousin Jessica, scowling at my feet, asked where I'd been I was able to answer, "To Miss Holly's house of course," in my most annoying voice and nothing more was said.

The next time I went to the river I felt much braver. The

water was quieter, and when I came to the stepping stones I helped myself across with a stick, and I did not slip in once. Then I started up the path on the other side. It was steep, and it looked a long way to the quarry. But before I was halfway up, there was a great scuffling and bounding behind me, and Waterloo caught up with me.

I was quite pleased to see him, but he was in a very bouncy mood, and at once he started racing ahead of me and back again, barking at any bird he saw and making so much noise and fuss that I was sure someone in the village below would notice us and tell Aunt Emma. So I turned back and ran down the hill, deciding that I must shut Waterloo into the garden shed before I went again.

Cousin Jessica very seldom left the house and garden and never went out of the village, so it was quite easy when she said, "Run out and play now, Merrie," to disappear for some time, but with Aunt Emma I had to be much more careful. She was apt to come to look for me if I stayed away for long.

One Saturday when we had been expecting my father for the weekend, there was a telephone call to say that he could not come. Aunt Emma went to see a friend in the next village and wouldn't take me, and Cousin Jessica was in a most tiresome mood, nagging at me for everything I did. Suddenly I made up my mind to run away. I'd make for one of the hill farms over the ridge in the next valley, miles and miles away!

I was so excited I could hardly wait for Cousin Jessica to drop off for her afternoon snooze. At last her head began to nod and I slipped out.

First I shut Waterloo into the garden shed, then I stuffed a hunk of cake and an apple into my pocket and started off along the lane. I meant to go up past the old quarry, through forbidden territory. There was a lovely mildness in the air though the trees were still bare.

I raced to the river, balanced carefully across the stepping stones and began to climb. My heart was light with excitement and with the lovely fresh earthy scents that rose all around me.

I got hotter and hotter as I puffed up the hill. I had to unbutton my coat and put my woolly cap into my pocket. Every now and then I stopped for a rest and looked down upon the village; blue smoke curled steadily up from the chimneys since there was no wind, and the road and the river slithered like a couple of silver snakes down the valley towards the lake.

The last bit of the path up to the quarry was very stony and steep. The sun had gone behind a cloud, and a mist seemed to be spreading and stretching down chilly fingers to grasp me.

I did not like being so very much alone, so far away from other people, but I plodded on, scrambling and slipping on the loose stones till I reached the hollowed circle of rock that long before had provided the building stone for the valley. The quarry was not in use any more. There was no call for it now, Aunt Emma said, with all those new-fangled flimsy houses.

I stood listening to the stillness. There was not even a sheep in sight and no bird stirred; the thin mist hung like a veil between me and the village. I puffed out my breath in a little cloud and tiny beads of mist clung to my coat and my hair. Then suddenly I felt I was no longer alone, someone or something was watching me. I took a deep breath and held it while my heart thumped loudly. My hair started to stiffen. For several seconds I did not dare to turn my head. When I did, I saw him at once.

He was leaning against a wall of stones, a kind of hut or shelter, just inside the quarry. He was a tall scarecrow of a man, his hair wild, his rough clothing frayed. I think if I had been able to, I'd have taken off down the hill like a rabbit, but I could not move, my legs were heavy as stone. We just stood and stared at one another till he spoke and then I was not frightened any more, my panic died away. His voice was soft, gentle.

"Have you come to see *me*, little bird?" he asked.

"Who are you?" I demanded, my courage returning.

"Giller Tyson," he replied.

"*Giller Tyson?*" I gasped. "But you *can't* be! He's the—" I had been going to say the Bogey-Man, remembering the game that the children in the village played, "Look out, or Giller Tyson will *get* you!"

"You'd better come in and rest a little," he invited me. "It's a long climb up from the village."

I followed him round the corner of the shelter wall, spell-bound, curious. We stepped down into a little hut built into the rock, a little room of stone. A turf fire burned in one corner and over it a black kettle hung from a hook. Along one wall there was a pile of dried bracken on which lay two neatly folded blankets. The room was very bare but clean and neat—somehow suitable.

I sat down on one of the blankets.

"Well, now you are safely in the Bogey-Man's den!" said Giller Tyson. We both burst out laughing.

3

"TAKE YOUR COAT OFF AND I'LL GET YOU A GLASS OF MILK,"
said Giller Tyson. "Did you come all the way from the village alone?"

"Yes," I said with satisfaction. "I'm running away and
I've always wanted to see the quarry—but I didn't expect to
find you here. Aunt Emma doesn't know I've come."

"Ah, you mean Miss Emma Eskin. Then you must be
Robert's child, I heard you had come to live with her."

"Yes, I'm Merrie, and my father's name is Robert. My
mother hasn't come to England. He left her behind in
Malaya," I astonished myself by telling him.

He held out a mug of milk to me and I took it and began
to drink, but it had a queer taste.

"It's goat's milk," he said. "Drink it up. It's good."

"Do other people come to see you, Mr. Tyson?" I asked.
"Aren't you lonely up here?"

"You can call me Giller," he said. "No, I have very few visitors, I don't encourage them. But I'm not lonely, I like it that way. I have my goat Selina for company. Next time you come, Merrie, I'll show her to you."

"Oh!" I cried. "*May* I come again—Giller?"

"Of course you may, but tell your Aunt Emma first so she knows where you are."

"Must I?" I asked. "I'd rather keep you a secret."

"Well, please yourself," he said. "Come now, I'll walk you down the hill a bit." He took my hand and I was glad, for the mist was thickening. I had forgotten all about running away.

"Why do they call you the Bogey-Man?" I asked.

"Perhaps because they're frightened of me. Also, I'm very particular about the company I choose. I like to be alone," he said.

"But you chose me, and you asked me to come again." I remarked with pleasure.

"Yes—but you are special, little bird," he said.

He took me across the stepping stones, then turned and without a word, strode off up the hill and disappeared into the mist.

I got back to the house before Aunt Emma, and Cousin Jessica asked no questions.

"Come along, dearie," she said. "I've made some scones for tea. Your eyes are shining and you look happy. You must have had a good game."

"Yes, I have," I said with satisfaction and I ran to wash my hands without being told.

I didn't tell Aunt Emma about Giller. I was afraid she might stop me from going because I had disobeyed her and crossed the river. And I couldn't risk not seeing him again. Besides, he was my secret.

About a week later, Cousin Jessica sent me to the shop for something she'd forgotten, and as I entered, Giller himself came striding out. There were other people about so he passed me without a sign of recognition except a quick wink and stalked off towards the river, a large sack slung over his shoulder—groceries no doubt.

"That's him! That's the Bogey-Man, Giller Tyson!" exclaimed two giggling little girls nudging me as I took my place in the shop beside them.

"I wonder who he's got in his sack?" said one little girl with awful glee.

"Silly, he's no Bogey-Man," I retorted. "Bogey-Men have terrible wicked faces—like this!" and I screwed up my face and squinted horribly.

Instead of going straight back with my shopping, I went the longer way round the back of the village to the river and stood watching Giller plodding up the hill on the other side, then I ran home along our lane.

When I got back, Aunt Emma was working in the front garden among masses of yellow flowers, and Cousin Jessica in the patch of vegetables outside the kitchen window.

"You can pick some daffodils for the house after tea," said Aunt Emma, "but not too many."

"I saw Giller Tyson in the village doing his shopping," I told her.

Aunt Emma stopped digging and gave me her full attention.

"*Did* you now," she said. "And what did you think of him?

"He's a nice man," I said. "It's silly to call him a Bogey-Man as the village children do."

"I agree with you, very silly," said Aunt Emma, and there was a sort of twinkle in her eye as she looked at me.

"How often does he come to the village? I've never seen him here before," I continued carefully.

"He comes for his provisions about once a week," said Aunt Emma. "He lives all alone on the mountain," she added.

"Does he *belong* to this village?" I asked next.

"Giller Tyson belongs to himself," said Aunt Emma. "But he grew up in this village, he and I were in the same class at school."

"Doesn't he work?" I asked.

"Not any more. He went to sea when he was young; he has been a sailor all his life. Now he has come home and he keeps himself to himself."

I felt I was on delicate ground, there was something in Aunt Emma's voice that warned me to ask no more questions. As she turned to resume her digging, I trailed into the kitchen swinging the basket of shopping for Cousin Jessica, and dumped it with a crash on the floor.

After tea I picked the daffodils and set them in a jar on the table, then I went upstairs to my room. I wanted to think about Giller, to sort out in my mind the things I knew about him. He must be older than I thought if he had been in the same class as Aunt Emma at school. And about him being a sailor—that interested me very much. I felt very excited about Giller, and I bounced up and down on my bed.

"I'll go up to see him again the next time Aunt Emma goes into town," I promised myself. "He's my best person here."

I looked out on the daffodils nodding under the apple trees—the tight apple blossom was almost ready to burst —and beyond to the fields and hills of green, green country where new lambs skipped about, bobbing their tails. The calling of the sheep to their lambs made a soothing kind of music, and I felt almost happy for the first time since I had come to England.

But my visit to Giller had to be postponed, for the next time Aunt Emma went into town, it was pouring rain. I did not dare cross the stepping stones over the swollen river, and it was too far to go round by the bridge.

Instead I brought my crayons and books and my teddy to the window alcove in the kitchen and began to play with them, while Cousin Jessica nodded in her chair by the fire, the pussy on her knee, and Waterloo stretched out under the table.

After a while there was a knock at the door, and Cousin Jessica woke with a start.

"Run and see who it is, Merrie," she said. I got up grumbling.

On the doorstep stood Mrs. Robinson from the farm. She wore gum boots and an old coat and her huge umbrella dripped all round her.

"Hello, Merrie. I've brought a few eggs for the house," she said.

I invited her inside and called to Cousin Jessica, then I went back to my game with Teddy—I had been telling him a story about a Bogey-Man.

Cousin Jessica brought Mrs. Robinson into the kitchen and sat her down by the fire. She made her a cup of tea, and they began to talk.

"Pay no attention to the child," whispered Cousin Jessica. "She's too busy with her game to hear us."

I went on telling Teddy the story as if this were true; but my ears were sharp and I could hear almost every word, though I only listened when there was something that interested me. The rain streamed down the windows; the clock ticked loudly; Waterloo whined in his dreams and the two old women, like a couple of pussy cats, gossiped together.

"That Giller Tyson came to the farm a few days back," said Mrs. Robinson and I pricked up my ears while I went on with Teddy's story. "Wanted a sack of potatoes dumped at the stepping stones for him—queer unfriendly sort he is."

"I never cared for him," Cousin Jessica replied. "Just as well *she* never married him. He'd have been no good to her."

"And broken her heart most likely," remarked Mrs. Robinson. "Well, well, it's an old story now."

I did not understand. Who would Giller have been no good to? Whose heart would he have broken? Silly old women, what did *they* know about Giller?

"How are things going with this one?" Mrs. Robinson then asked, nodding sideways towards me and lowering her voice a little.

"Oh, she's settling quite nicely now," said Cousin Jessica. "Children soon forget, that's what I always say. She seems quite contented, but she's a queer, touchy little thing, you know, very secretive and solitary."

"Must have been terrible hard for her to leave her mother all the same," said Mrs. Robinson, "no wonder she's touchy. Maybe she would have been better left behind, too."

"Emma wouldn't have it," said Cousin Jessica. "She insisted on Robert's bringing his child home with him. Of course the mother couldn't come, it wouldn't have been suitable, you know. They weren't married, and in any case she wouldn't leave her own country. Emma is quite right, the child is better off here."

The voices droned on, but I didn't hear any more. I wished I had not listened. I only partly understood what they had been saying, but I did not want to hear any more of such hurting disturbing things. I tried to forget them. I wished my father had left me in Malaya, it would have been kinder to let me grow up among my own people. No one really wanted me in England, no one cared about me—unless perhaps Giller.

I went up to visit him a few days later and that time Waterloo accompanied me.

"So you've come back, little bird," he said when I reached the edge of the quarry and called out to him. "I'm glad to see you."

He introduced me to Selina, his goat, and he showed me his rock garden in the shelter of the quarry. "Wait till the flowers are out, in a month's time. You won't know it in its spring colors." I could see that he, too, loved flowers; he was so fond of his garden.

I sat in his hut, and we talked seriously together.

"I do not love my father," I told him. "He says my mother is going to be married and doesn't want me any more. Why didn't my father leave me behind in Malaya? At least I'd have had a place there in my grandmother's *kampong*."

"Perhaps he loved you too much to leave you behind," Giller suggested.

I didn't believe him! "Well nobody here cares about me!" I shouted, suddenly angry.

"That's not true," said Giller quietly. "I care about you, your Aunt Emma cares about you. You can make a place for yourself here with us, little bird, if you want to."

4

WHEN THE SUMMER CAME, WITH LONG WARM DAYS, AND the sun shone in the green valley and the flowers came out, I began to feel much more alive. I was able to leave off my thick clothes and heavy shoes, my nose stopped feeling pinched with cold, and my skin no longer looked gray. Once or twice my father came for weekends, and Aunt Emma and Cousin Jessica twittered with pleasure as they fussed over him. But between him and me there was a wall. I did not trust him, and although he brought me presents from London and took me out in his car by myself for a treat, I was edgy and wary with him.

"Aren't you going to thank your father for the storybook he brought you?" asked Aunt Emma.

"No," I retorted, "I don't want it." But secretly in my room I looked at its pictures over and over again, cherishing it.

After he had gone I felt sorry and wished I had made friends with him. "Next time it will be different," I said.

I must have looked woebegone, for Aunt Emma gave me one of her rare hugs. "Cheer up, dearie," she said. "Your father is coming back quite soon to spend his summer holiday here with us—two weeks, and he's bringing a friend with him. *Two weeks*, won't that be lovely?"

"Yes," I replied. "Two weeks might be long enough."

"Long enough for what?" asked Aunt Emma.

"To get to know one another, inside our skins," I said, and I thought of all the questions I wanted to ask him. Aunt Emma looked astonished as if I had said something outrageous.

"What a strange little girl you are," she remarked. "You must know Robert inside out already—he's your *father*."

Soon lessons finished till the autumn, and the long summer days were warm and stretched invitingly ahead.

Aunt Emma allowed me to run wild while the unusual spell of hot weather lasted. I went with some of the local children to help with the hay making on the farms or to watch the sheep being clipped and dipped or to paddle in the shallows in the river while the bigger children dived and swam in the deep pools. I enjoyed being one of this village band. I enjoyed the fun and the laughter, but I did not allow any of them to come too close to me. I did not make a personal friend of any of them. As often as I could, I slipped away unnoticed and climbed the hill to Giller's hut. There I would spend a happy hour or two sitting on the turf beside him while he worked away at his wood carving—strange little shapes, half animal, half human, mushrooms with faces, gnomelike tree creatures, which he sold to the tourist shops in town. Aunt Emma did not question me about where I'd been, and for this I was grateful, nor did she ask me if I'd ever crossed the river.

Day after day the sun shone down, not a scorching but a gentle sun, and everyone in the village remarked on the astonishingly fine summer.

"No rain for six weeks now," said Cousin Jessica. "We'll be having a drought soon. Be sure to turn the taps off, Merrie." I often left them running just to annoy her.

Before the day of my father's arrival, there were great preparations made by the two old women. The house shone with polish, and delicious smells of good things to eat lingered about the kitchen.

"We'll put Robert in his own room, of course," Aunt Emma said, and I knew she meant the room that had been his as a boy. "But what about his friend? D'you think the little room is too small for him? Had we better put him in the attic bedroom on the top floor?"

"Oh no, no," said Cousin Jessica. "He'll be all right in the little room next to Merrie. He's young isn't he?"

Aunt Emma laughed. "I suppose so," she said, "but I don't really know anything about him. Robert only said he'd like to bring a friend—you know how vague he can be."

I sat on the front step beside Waterloo waiting for the car to arrive. I was full of hope. Surely everything was going to be all right this time. I kept a sharp lookout through the apple trees in the garden to the road beyond. The car would have to come up the lane at the side of the house and garden to the yard at the back where the garage was, so I'd have plenty of time to warn Aunt Emma when they appeared.

Suddenly there was the sound of a horn and my father's car turned into the lane, drove slowly up it and stopped at the little gate at the side of the house.

"They've come!" I yelled to Aunt Emma, and I jumped up, and with Waterloo barking his head off, raced to the lane. Outside the gate, I hesitated, waiting for my father to unfold himself as he got out of the car, uncertain of his mood. But he held out his arms to me and joyfully I jumped into them and clung to him. It was not until he set me down that I remembered his friend and turned to the other side of the car. A tall slim figure was just getting out —a *girl*, a lovely girl with hair the color of pale sunshine!

"Hello, Merrie," she said holding out her hand to me.

I shook hands politely. I put on my smiling face, but inside I was scowling and angry. What was this strange girl doing here? Why had she come? What had she to do with *my* father?

By this time, Aunt Emma and Cousin Jessica had arrived to join in the welcome.

"This is my friend, Bergit Ericson," said my father proudly. "She is Norwegian, but she's working over here."

I could see by her face that Cousin Jessica was as surprised as I was, though Aunt Emma managed to hide what she felt.

"Come along in, my dear," she said taking the girl by the arm. "Robert will bring your case. Tea is on the table."

It was a very special tea. The scones and cakes and biscuits Cousin Jessica had baked looked wonderfully tempting; but although my father and the girl ate huge amounts, I didn't feel hungry and couldn't manage to swallow more than one biscuit, and that nearly choked me.

"Come on, Merrie," cried Cousin Jessica. "What's happened to your appetite? You're usually so hungry for your tea."

"Aren't you feeling well?" my father asked.

I nodded my head. "Yes," I said, "I'm quite well thank

you, but I'm not hungry."

"Perhaps she's had too much sun?" the girl suggested, but my father laughed at that.

"Not Merrie," he said. "You forget where she's from. This English sun is nothing to her."

The girl blushed and looked uncomfortable as if she had said something stupid, and I felt more kindly towards her. She had meant to be friendly.

Aunt Emma came to my aid. "If you don't want any more tea, dearie," she said, "perhaps you'd like to go out to play in the garden."

I slipped off my chair and ran outside and up into my tree house to hide from them all.

The day was spoiled. I felt cheated and sick with disappointment. The plans I had made for the two weeks of my father's holiday were ruined. Now everything would be different, and all because of this girl. Why did she have to come?

When she and my father came out of the house together, I ground my teeth as I watched them stroll out of the gate, down the lane, and take the path up the hill on the other side of the valley. I was forgotten already. I stayed hidden till Aunt Emma came into the orchard and gently called for me to come to the farm with her for eggs. But although I came down from my tree house, I would not go with her, and after she had gone off without me, I wandered into the kitchen. Cousin Jessica had washed up the tea things and was putting the cakes and biscuits away in tins.

"Perhaps you'd like one now?" she said, offering me the plate. "What a silly little girl you are."

It was all that was needed to spark me off.

"No! I'd hate one!" I screamed. "And why do you call me silly? Silly old woman yourself!" I snatched a little cake from the plate and threw it at her. I stamped my foot at her and banged on the table, clattering the cups and plates in their tidy piles. Cousin Jessica looked astonished, then shocked and even a little frightened, and I was glad! Before she could get hold of me I fled from the kitchen, out of the house and onto the main road. I ran along it, which was quite forbidden, in the direction of the farm, and reached the stile into the field just as Aunt Emma appeared on the other side of it.

She climbed over the stile and we crossed the road together and entered the lane to the farm, then she took my hand.

"So you came after all," she said gently. "You should have come by the field, though, not by the road, you know. It's shorter and safer."

"I know," I said. "I'm sorry, and I was rude to Cousin Jessica before I came out, too."

"You'll feel better tomorrow, dearie," said Aunt Emma. "Dry your tears. Bergit seems a nice girl. You'll like her when you're used to her." Then as an afterthought she said, "I think you're old enough to cross the river now by yourself, but be careful at the stepping stones and don't wander too far."

I squeezed her hand. I felt as if she had given me wings. Perhaps Aunt Emma understood me better than I had given her credit for.

5

For the two weeks of my father's holiday he and the girl, Bergit, were inseparable. It was a long time since I had seen him so happy. Sometimes they took me in the car with them, sometimes Aunt Emma and Cousin Jessica came, too, but more often they went off alone together leaving me behind. I was torn in two, one part of me longing to be accepted and loved by them, the other wanting to hurt and destroy their happiness. The girl, Bergit, attracted me strongly. If I could have overcome my jealousy of her, I would have liked to have made friends with her, but when she tried to approach me, I rebuffed her, staring at her with hostile eyes.

If it had not been for Giller, that time would have been much worse for me. When I was with him, I was happy. I visited his hut as often as I could. He was the one person I trusted, in his friendship I felt safe and cherished. Sometimes I worked with him in his rock garden, sometimes I played with Selina. He taught me how to milk her. But the best times of all were when he told me stories, wonderful stories of places he had seen as he sailed round the world, of people he had known, of homes he had visited. I could never hear enough of Giller's tales, but he had to be persuaded and cajoled into telling them, even to me. He kept them locked up inside his head, like precious jewels. "Riches of the mind," he called them. "All stored here, ready to take out and enjoy when I please. Those are riches worth having, Merrie. No one can take them away from me."

I felt he was trying to tell me something, something important he wanted me to remember.

Near the end of my father's holiday, the weather changed, the fine spell began to break up. One day, when I got back from Giller's hut, ominous black clouds were massing behind the mountains, spreading across the sky, and there was a kind of breathlessness in Aunt Emma's house. I knew we were in for a storm. I had got back just in time because the first rumbles of thunder were beginning.

"Come here a minute, Merrie," my father called and I ran into the sitting room. Aunt Emma was there and Bergit with my father. I went and stood by his knee.

Bergit turned to me and held out her hand. "Merrie, your father and I are going to be married soon," she said, "and you'll come to live with us later on I hope."

So *that* was it. I looked from one to the other in silence. "I don't care," I said coldly, and I turned to leave the room.

But at that moment there was a tremendous clap of thunder overhead and lightning spat in a blue zigzag. I gave a yell of panic and ran sobbing to bury my face in Aunt Emma's lap.

"She has always hated thunder," said my father.

"It's all right," said Aunt Emma stroking my hair, "its all right, dearie, the storm's nearly over." When the storm ended, I trudged my way upstairs and carefully shut the door of my room. But not before I heard one comment.

"A little dark thorn," murmured Bergit, but her voice was gentle so I was not as offended as I might have been.

I thought it all over when I was in bed that night. It was true what I had said, I did not care about my father and Bergit getting married. What I *did* care about was leaving Giller.

The next day, after they had gone, I climbed the hillside to the quarry to tell Giller, but he already knew.

"I'll be leaving here, Giller," I said, "after they're married."

"But that won't be for quite a time," he said reassuringly, "and you'll be better off in a home of your own with your father—we're all too old for you here, little bird. She sounds like an unusual girl, that Bergit, and kind; you'll grow fond of her, I shouldn't wonder. She comes from a beautiful land, grander than ours and wilder, from a brave adventurous people, a people used to hardship and danger." He went on to tell me of the old Norsemen, the Vikings he called them, who long ago had sailed across the stormy seas in their dragon-headed ships to explore and raid other, richer lands. Sea robbers they were. I listened spellbound to his tale, and somehow it made me think differently of Bergit. My interest was aroused, and I began to want to know more about her.

A few days later the engagement was announced in the papers and Cousin Jessica pointed it out to me.

"Bergit will make a good wife for your father," she said, "and see that you behave yourself when you go to live with them, missie." As soon as she turned her back, I put out my tongue at her, silly old pussy cat Jessica!

The next morning when the post came, there was a letter for me. I couldn't believe my eyes. I had never had a letter before. Aunt Emma gave it to me at breakfast and I turned it over and over in my hands, feeling it and trying to guess what was inside it and who had sent it. The writing was small and neat and it had a pretty stamp. I propped it up in front of me on the table and went on eating.

"Aren't you going to open it to see who it's from?" asked Cousin Jessica, her eyes popping with curiosity.

"No, not yet," I answered, and I folded it in half and tucked it into my pocket, away from her prying eyes.

"Well," she said pursing up her fat little mouth, "you *are* a queer child."

Aunt Emma said nothing and after breakfast when she went up to make her bed, I followed her upstairs to my room. Carefully, so as not to tear it, I opened the envelope and spread out the sheet of paper on the windowsill. I pored over it for some time, trying to make out what it said, but the writing was too difficult for me. Even if it had been printed, my reading was not yet very good. So I went across the passage and knocked at Aunt Emma's door.

"Come in, Merrie," she called. "I thought you might want me. Is it your letter?"

"Yes," I said, shutting the door behind me. "Please will you read it to me?"

Aunt Emma put on her glasses and took it from my hand. "It's from Bergit," she told me, "and this is what she says:

" 'Dear Merrie,

I enjoyed staying in Aunt Emma's house and meeting you. Your father had told me so much about you. I am going home to *my* father and mother in Norway soon. Then when I come back to England, we will be getting married and finding a house of our own. Later on, when we are settled in, I hope you will come and live with us. Aunt Emma will miss you, I know, but she has Cousin Jessica; and when your father is away at work all day, I shall be all alone, so I hope you will come and keep me company, please? Your father, too, wants to have you with him again.

I send my love to you and Aunt Emma and Cousin Jessica and Waterloo.

From Bergit.' "

Aunt Emma gave it back to me, and I sighed with pleasure as I folded it and put it back into its envelope.

"That's a very nice letter, dearie," said Aunt Emma. "You'll be lucky to have Bergit for your mother."

"She'll never be my *mother*," I retorted, stung, and I jumped up and ran out of the room slamming the door. But it was Aunt Emma I was angry with, not Bergit. Her letter pleased me very much, she was inviting me to live with them in their new home, not ordering me, and I felt grateful to her for treating me like a person. I wondered where I could hide her letter, safe from Cousin Jessica's prowlings? Then I remembered the snakeskin bag I had brought from Malaya. Cousin Jessica was terrified of snakes, she had told me so. I took the bag out of the drawer where I kept it, popped the letter inside it, drew tight the strings and hung it in my cupboard where it dangled among my clothes. I hoped it would scare her if she found it!

6

Soon after this it was my birthday and Aunt Emma said I could ask three friends to tea, and Cousin Jessica said she'd bake me a cake with seven candles.

I did not know which of the children to ask to tea. I had no special friend. The only person I wanted to ask was Giller, and that was impossible; he was a secret. But to please Aunt Emma, I invited three of the children I played with: Johnny Stone, the doctor's son; the baker's boy, David Bland; and Duncan Robinson from the farm.

"What? All boys? No little girls?" asked Cousin Jessica, and I knew she was just about to remark as usual what a *queer* little girl I was, when Aunt Emma cut in. "I said she could ask whom she pleased," she said. "Why do you like boys best, dearie?"

"Because girls—*bother* me," I said, and Aunt Emma chuckled as if she understood what I meant.

When the day of my birthday arrived, it was sunless and chilly with a promise of rain in the wind.

I stretched up to my full height before the mirror, hoping that I might have grown in the night, but I had not changed; I was still small for my age.

Beside my plate at breakfast time there were two parcels. I read my name on them.

Aunt Emma gave me a story book with lovely pictures and promised to read it to me, and from Cousin Jessica there was a pair of bright red woolen gloves that she had knitted for me. Two parcels—and that was all. Nothing from my father, not yet, but there was another post later on. There was sure to be something from him then.

I had hoped to climb the hill and see Giller, but Aunt Emma wanted me to walk with her to the farm to get the eggs. In the afternoon the boys were coming, so the visit to Giller had to wait till the next day.

Mrs. Robinson, the farmer's wife, invited us into the kitchen and while Aunt Emma had a cup of tea, I had a glass of milk and some of Mrs. Robinson's gingerbread.

"Duncan's away with the men," she said to me, "but he'll be back in good time for your party this afternoon, Merrie. Gracie's collecting the eggs in the yard if you'd like to go and help her."

"Oh yes," I cried, and I ran outside. I liked Gracie, she was not quite a grown-up.

When we visited each nesting box, Gracie let me put my hand in and lift out the smooth brown eggs, sometimes only one, but often there were three or four waiting to be collected. But when we found a hen sitting in a box, I dared not put my hand in for fear the hen would peck me, and Gracie had to do it. Her big basket was half-full of eggs when we had finished.

"Go and fetch your aunt's basket," said Gracie when we reached the dairy, "and find out how many eggs she wants."

I took Aunt Emma's basket to Gracie. "One dozen please," I said. Then I ran back to Aunt Emma in the kitchen to finish my milk and gingerbread.

When Gracie brought our basket of eggs, there was a very large one resting on a leaf on the top.

"That one is for you, Merrie," said Gracie. "Happy Birthday!"

I lifted it out carefully. It was a huge egg. Gracie had drawn a face on it and hair, and on the back of it was printed "Merrie."

"Oh thank you," I cried, delighted. "It's a lovely present, Gracie." Now I had three birthday presents, and when the parcel post came I was sure there would be another one from my father.

When we got back to Aunt Emma's house, the post had not arrived, so I climbed on to the garden wall and sat there watching the road for the red van to make sure that I did not miss it. Waterloo jumped up and lay along the wall beside me as if he knew it was my birthday but could give me nothing but his company.

Before long I saw the postman's van coming towards the village, and as it came nearer I began to wave so that it was sure to stop.

"Good morning Merrie," the postman called as he drew up on the other side of the road.

"Please, is there a parcel for me?" I asked eagerly.

"You got a birthday or something?" he asked. I nodded, and he started to look through a small pile of parcels on the seat beside him. He began to shake his head as he finished reading the names on them.

"Sorry, Merrie," he said. "Nothing for you today—perhaps it'll come tomorrow."

He reached into the pocket by the driving wheel. "Here, happy birthday," he cried and he tossed me a packet of toffees before he drove off. I opened it and put one into my mouth; it was very good, and I gave one to Waterloo. It stuck his teeth together so that he dribbled all down his fur and looked so funny that I couldn't help laughing. But for me the day was spoiled, there was no parcel from my father, he had forgotten my birthday, he didn't care. I was miserable.

I went in and got my egg from the basket, and I stood it in an egg cup on a shelf of the kitchen dresser so that it would be safe.

After dinner I badly wanted to go and see Giller, but I knew I had no time before the boys came, so I went up to my room.

Out of my drawer I took the clothes I had worn before I came to England, black trousers and a little cotton coat with gold buttons. When I put them on, they were too tight for me, the legs and sleeves a little short, so that I knew I must have grown a bit and I was pleased. I took a flower from the vase on the dressing table and wore it in my hair. Then I sat on the floor and pretended I was in my grandmother's house, as I had been on my last birthday, and that she and my mother were with me and many of our friends from the village. For half an hour I was home in Malaya again, talking and laughing with my own people, acting the ceremony of my birthday party. I took my gold bangle from my wrist and wrapped it in paper and pretended that it was my mother's birthday present to me. I helped myself to make-believe dishes of cakes and sweets and drank fruit juice from grandmother's best cups.

When it was over and I put on my English clothes and

my English ways again, I felt comforted, and the hurt of my father's negligence was eased a little.

Soon the boys arrived, each one had brought me a present of sweets, and we ran out into the garden to play and climb the trees. Cousin Jessica had provided a splendid tea, crowned by a beautiful iced birthday cake with seven candles.

After tea, as it was a gray and chilly afternoon, Aunt Emma let us help her make a bonfire in the rubbish patch in the garden, and we had a lovely time burning up the clippings and prunings and dead flowers that had collected for weeks.

When the boys had gone, Aunt Emma sent me upstairs to wash and get tidy for supper. As soon as I was alone, I began to fret again that my father had forgotten my birthday. "Perhaps his parcel will come tomorrow," I told myself. "Perhaps it got left behind in the post," but I did not feel very hopeful.

The supper bell rang and I ran downstairs, into the kitchen where Aunt Emma and Cousin Jessica were already seated at the table. And on my plate, in its egg cup, its face all smudged and its top bashed in, stood my beautiful egg that Gracie had given me! Cousin Jessica had boiled it for my supper!

I was furiously angry!

I let out a howl of rage and turned on her.

"How *dare* you touch my egg without asking me!" I shouted. "It's mine and I didn't want it boiled. You've spoiled it, and I hate you!" I rushed at her and began to hit her and scratch her, kicking out at her in a fury.

Then I started to scream. Aunt Emma pulled me back and slapped my face.

"Stop it, Merrie," she said, "stop it at once and sit down."

She gripped my shoulders and pushed me on to my chair. Then she removed the egg out of sight. I slumped down, whimpering, and began to kick the table leg, still rebellious.

"What a disgraceful exhibition!" Cousin Jessica exclaimed.

"We'll not discuss it just now," said Aunt Emma crisply, and she began to talk about something quite different.

I had to apologize to Cousin Jessica later, and Aunt Emma gave me a lecture about losing my temper.

"Cousin Jessica meant to please you," Aunt Emma explained. "She did not mean any harm."

"She should have asked me," I retorted. "The egg was *mine*. But I suppose she can't help being stupid. She doesn't really know about children, does she?"

"She's never had any children," said Aunt Emma, as if that explained everything.

"Nor have you," I replied, "but you're not like that."

"Ah, but I had your father," said Aunt Emma smiling. "He lived with me from the time he was ten when his parents died, and he was just like my own son." I found it difficult to think of my father growing up in Aunt Emma's house—in fact I found it difficult to think of my father as a boy at all.

Next morning was misty, but I set off early for Giller's hut. On the way, I stopped at the river's edge and carefully selected a smooth stone of the shape and size of my egg, and I put it into my pocket.

"I've got a surprise for you," said Giller as soon as he saw me. "Come in by the fire and I'll fetch it. Yesterday was your birthday, wasn't it?"

"Why, yes," I said, "but how did you know?"

"There are lots of things I know, little bird," he said teasingly. "Now sit down and shut your eyes."

I felt him place something on my knee, and when I

opened my eyes, I found a little wooden chest like a miniature trunk, painted in bright colors with flowers and animals. It even had a lock with a tiny key.

"Oh!" I exclaimed. "What a beautiful present. Did you make it for me?"

Giller nodded. "In Norway, the old custom was for every bride to have a big painted chest like this tiny one, in which she kept her linen. You see them in the houses or farms in the country still. The bride's initials and the date would be on the outside—see, I have put your initials on yours."

I examined the chest carefully and saw the letters M.E. for Meriam Eskin, each letter surrounded by a little garland of daisies.

"Oh thank you, Giller!" I said. "It is very beautiful." And suddenly I was happy. I didn't mind so much that my father had forgotten my birthday, for Giller cared.

I hung the little key on a piece of string round my neck and went out to find Selina.

Before I left to go back to Aunt Emma's house, I took the stone from my pocket and told Giller about my egg.

"Will you paint a face on my stone for me?" I asked him.

"You can use my paints and do it yourself," he said. When it was done, I put it in my pocket. I was very pleased with it, it made me laugh. "I will call it 'Gom,' " I said.

I had to get Giller's present safely into Aunt Emma's house without anyone seeing it, for nobody knew of my visits to Giller.

So when I had crossed the river by the stepping stones, I took off my parka and carried it over my arm with the little chest wrapped inside it. No one saw me come in, although Cousin Jessica heard me and called, "Is that you, Merrie?" I paid no attention and reached my room safely. There I hid my lovely present in the cupboard where I hung my clothes.

7

THE PRESENT FROM MY FATHER ARRIVED A WEEK LATER,
when I had given up all hope that he would remember my
birthday. I had waited and been disappointed for too long,
and when the parcel *did* arrive, I had no joy in it. He had
sent me a leather school satchel to wear slung round my
shoulder when I went to the village school—the big school
—in September.

Inside the satchel there was a small parcel from Bergit, a
little embroidered apron she had made for me. The fact
that she had made something for me herself pleased me. It
was a very pretty apron and when I wore it on one of my
visits to Giller, he told me that he had seen Norwegian
women working on embroidery just like it.

It was a mild day in early September, and as we sat talking outside Giller's hut, Selina wandered about close to us
as if she liked our company.

"School begins tomorrow," I told Giller. "I am going to the big school you know."

The big school lay half a mile or so further up the valley, and was shared by our village and two smaller ones, and children also came from the outlying farms. There were about thirty children between the ages of five and eleven.

"Do you know any of the children who go there? Will you have friends to go with?" Giller asked.

"Some," I answered uncertainly, and my hand in my pocket tightened round my stone, my Gom.

"You'll be all right," said Giller reassuringly. "And if I hear of anyone bothering you, they'll have me, the Bogey-Man to reckon with!" He made a fierce face, and we both burst out laughing.

It was all right to start with. Aunt Emma was too much respected in the village for there to be any real trouble. Also, in spite of my small size, I could run and climb trees as well as anyone of my age, and this surprised some of them. And I was quick-witted. I could prick and sting with words better than any of them. I could fight, too, if I had to. But there was one boy, Sammy Green, who loved to tease and plague me. He was in the class above me and bigger than I was and I hated him. He called me brown face. Although I always found comfort in the thought that I had only to tell Giller and he would deal with Sammy, I did not tell him. I wanted to fight my own battles. Wherever I went at that time, I carried my stone, Gom, with me. It had become a sort of good luck charm that gave me courage and security.

One day when we came out of school and I parted from my friends at the crossroads, Sammy and two of his mates were waiting for me at the field gate.

"Come here, Merrie, brown face," said Sammy. "There's something we want to ask you."

"I haven't time," I retorted warily. But the three of them quickly surrounded me, Sammy took me by the arms and hustled me off the road and into the field behind its stone wall.

I had been frightened, but now a wild burst of anger shook me and my right hand went into my pocket to grasp Gom tightly.

"How dare you touch me, fat Sammy Green!" I shouted. "Let me go at once or I'll bash you! I'll tell the Bogey-Man on you!"

They greeted this with howls of laughter, which made me wilder than ever.

"Oh you will, will you?" said Sammy. "O.K. you tell him. But first we want to know—what do you carry in your pocket, Merrie?"

His voice was soft, taunting, but dangerous and his eyes sparkled with malice. I glared back at him furiously.

"I'll show you!" I shouted and grasping Gom in my hand I whipped it out of my pocket and quick as lightning, I hit him full on his nose and then on his forehead, twice.

It took him completely by surprise. Blood poured from his nose, his face went white, and he collapsed on the grass edge of the lane where his friends bent anxiously over him.

My temper died. I was frightened at what I had done, and before any of them recovered their wits, I turned into the road and raced for Aunt Emma's house.

I said nothing about what had happened, and after tea Aunt Emma went out on some errand.

She did not get back till almost supper time and as soon as she came in, she told me to come to her room. Her face was very stern as she made me stand before her.

"You'd better tell me what happened this afternoon," she said.

So I told her—some.

"That's not all," she said. "What was in your hand? You couldn't have hurt him so much with only your fist."

I put my hand into my pocket and drew out Gom and held it out to her.

"I didn't really mean to damage him," I said, "at least not badly. It just—happened."

Aunt Emma took my stone and examined it thoughtfully.

"You mean you lost your temper and hurt him more than you meant to?" she asked.

I glared back at her. "I'm glad I hurt him. He's always calling me brown face," I said. "I know now that I hit him harder than I should have, but at the time—I'd like to have *killed* him!"

"You might have done just that," said Aunt Emma quietly. "It was wicked and dangerous to use a stone however much he teased and annoyed you. Fight with your fists if you must, but never, *never* with a stone. Can't you see how dangerous it is to lose your temper, to lose control of yourself so that you don't know what you are doing?"

I glared back at her but acknowledged inwardly that the violence of my rage had frightened even me.

"I ought to take your stone away from you," Aunt Emma continued, "but I'm not going to—*this* time. The stone means something important to you, doesn't it? But let me warn you, if ever you fight with it again, I will take it from you for ever. Will you promise me to try to control your temper and never again to hit anyone with a stone in your hand?"

I stood silent for a moment thinking.

"All right," I said. "I promise."

"And you'll have to come round with me, now, to

Sammy Green's home and apologize to him," she added.

"Well," I said, "if I do, *he* should apologize for torment-ing me."

"Yes, perhaps he will," said Aunt Emma. "Come along, we'll go at once."

Sammy Green's face was a sorry sight. There was a great pad of cotton wool plastered across his nose and a huge swollen lump on his forehead. But I didn't feel one bit sorry for him, I felt pleased with myself.

Aunt Emma and Sammy's mother were friends and must have come to an agreement about us for when I apologized to him, we were made to shake hands and Sammy promised to stop teasing me.

I never had any more trouble with him. In fact, he kept well away from me. But the story of my fight with him was spread around, and I found it earned me some respect and gave me some importance in the school. As long as I re-mained there, I was never mocked nor tormented by any-one again. I still carried Gom around with me, but I kept my promise to Aunt Emma, I didn't fight with it.

8

When Christmas came, my father and Bergit arrived to stay in Aunt Emma's house. Snow lay deep and thick on every side. Sunlight sparkled on the white fields and hills, and all the children of the village spent the days tobogganing on trays or homemade sleds. When the sun began to dip behind the mountains, we hurried home tired and contented and ravenous for tea. Deep blue shadows lay upon the fells and the familiar woods and lanes, making them places of mystery. The brooks were frozen into cascades of ice, and even the river banks hung with icicles. The patterns made by the frost on my window were lovely as the flowers at home in Malaya, and at night when I lay in bed, the stars seemed near enough to touch. I loved the stillness brought by the snow; the hooting of an owl in the darkness or the light bark of a fox took on a new sound, a quality of magic.

For a whole week I did not see Giller; the snow was too

deep for me to climb the hill to his hut. Then one morning when I had been to the shop for Cousin Jessica, I met him striding up the road towards the farm, his sack over his shoulder.

"Well, little bird," he said. "How do you like this white world?"

"I like it very much," I answered, "except that I can't get up the hill to see you. Is your hut all right, or are you cold?"

"I keep a good fire going," said Giller. "We are very comfortable, Selina and I, until our food runs out and I have to come down to get some more." He turned and looked up the hillside towards the old quarry.

"It's a pity you can't *fly* up to visit us," he said. "It's a wider world up there; a man can see farther."

"I'll come up when the snow is gone," I promised. "Give my love to Selina."

"Oh! I nearly forgot—this is for you," he said, and putting his hand in his pocket, he took out a tiny squirrel he had carved out of wood for me. It looked so like a real one it might have been alive, poised ready to spring to the next branch.

"Oh, thank you," I cried. "Thank you very much. It's lovely. I will keep it in my treasure chest, the one you made me for my birthday. I must hurry now, Cousin Jessica is waiting for this margarine to make a pie for dinner."

"Goodbye then. Don't come up till the snow has gone," said Giller, hitching his sack on his shoulder.

I ran back with the basket and burst into the kitchen, forgetting to stamp the snow off my feet.

"I'm going to build a snowman in the garden," I cried, setting the basket on the table.

"Out you go, out of my clean kitchen," Cousin Jessica shouted good-humoredly, and Bergit, who was peeling potatoes at the sink, asked, "Shall I come and help you when I've finished these?"

"If you want to," I said, but I was pleased. I was beginning to like Bergit. She treated me as if I were a *person*. I decided to show her my squirrel later on.

When I got into bed that night, I put the squirrel into my wooden chest and hid it under my blankets. Outside my window, the splendid snowman Bergit and I had made stood stiffly on guard. When she came to say good night to me, I felt quite friendly towards her, so I showed her my squirrel and my treasure chest.

"You mustn't tell *anyone*," I warned her, "no one else has seen them."

"Where did you get them from?" Bergit asked. "This little chest is Norwegian; we have lots like this in Norway only bigger. My mother has one in her house."

I felt tempted to tell her about Giller, but I decided not to. I was not sure yet how far I could trust her, so I just said, "My friend gave them to me, made them for me, but you're not to tell anyone."

"I won't, I promise," said Bergit, "and thank you for showing them to me." She bent to kiss me good night, but I dived under my blankets and hid my face from her. I was not ready to let myself love her yet.

"Will you write another letter to me when you go away?" I called just before she left the room.

"Yes, of course I will," she promised. "Good night, Merrie."

When she had gone, I lay in the darkness thinking of her, then of Giller. I hoped the snow would disappear soon, beautiful though it was, so that I could get up the hill to the quarry.

When Bergit and my father were married and I went to

live with them, I would have to leave Giller. Perhaps I'd
never see him again! How could I bear it? It never entered
my head that Giller might leave *me*.

They were married in London at Easter time, my father
and Bergit, and when Aunt Emma told me, I asked her how
soon I'd be going to live with them.

"They haven't found a house of their own yet," said Aunt
Emma, "so it might be September before you go, or even
Christmas time, or you might be here for another year.
There's no hurry, is there?"

I sighed with relief that I hadn't to go at once. "No," I
said, smiling, "there's no hurry."

Aunt Emma put her arms round me and gave me a shy
hug and I let her. I knew she was pleased that I was in no
hurry to leave her. She could not guess that it was because
of Giller I was glad to stay longer.

Early in May, after a month of mild spring weather, there
was a sudden cold spell and we had a freak snow storm. The
apple and cherry blossoms were hung with great tufts of
snow, and the daffodil heads were bowed to the ground
with its weight. But it only lasted for a day and was gone,
and I was able to climb the wet hillside to visit Giller.

Waterloo came with me, bounding ahead of me, delighted to be alive.

The path was slippery with mud and it took me longer
than usual to reach the old quarry. I called out, as I always
did, in a rather breathless voice, but there was no answering
call from Giller and he did not appear. Either he had not
heard me or else he was out. I called again more loudly as I
stumbled over the rough stones to his hut and pushed open
the door. Giller lay quite still on the floor. His eyes were
closed. His face was twisted and he breathed with a loud

kind of snoring. At least he was alive!

"Giller!" I cried despairingly as I fell on my knees beside him. "Giller! Speak to me. Giller! Giller!"

I seized his hand and tugged at it, hoping to rouse him, but it felt cold against my cheek and dropped limply when I let it go. Something dreadful had happened to him; he might die if I didn't go and get help at once! Yet how could I leave him?

I pulled the blankets off his bed and tucked them round him and I folded his coat and put it under his head. He did not move nor open his eyes. Then I remembered Waterloo. "Stay with him. Sit!" I ordered. The good dog lay down, softly whining, beside him. I turned for the door, shut it behind me, and raced down the hill as I'd never run before. Slithering and sliding, and falling several times, I reached the bottom at last. I ran through the river—there was no time for stepping stones—and came gasping and exhausted to the lane. I ran on past Aunt Emma's, up the road to the doctor's house. I threw myself like a wild thing against his door. I couldn't reach the knocker and the bell didn't ring, so I pulled Gom out of my pocket and battered with it on the door. The doctor came at once, but I was so breathless and upset, I could hardly speak.

"It's Giller . . . he's lying on the floor of his hut up there in the quarry . . . he's dreadfully ill," I gasped.

"Giller Tyson? Did he send you for me?" the doctor asked.

"No, I found him, he didn't send me, he can't speak. His eyes are shut and he looks terrible, but he's not dead because he's breathing in a queer way. Oh hurry, please hurry!" I cried desperately.

"Go straight back to your aunt," said the doctor, "and tell her what's happened. I'll go to Giller at once. You're a good girl, Merrie." He patted my shoulder.

He picked up his bag and ran to the garage, and in a moment he was tearing down the road in his car, making for the shallows in the river by the stepping stones. My legs had gone wobbly and I couldn't run any more, but when I reached our lane, his car was just crossing the river so I knew he must have decided on the way to stop at Aunt Emma's house.

She was speaking on the telephone as I got in. ". . . at once, send it at *once*, it's urgent." She listened for a moment as I stood by her. "Yes, that's right, the old quarry. Dr. Stone says to hurry."

She rang off and turned to me, and I saw she was shaking.

"They're sending an ambulance from the hospital, and men to carry him down the hill," she said. Then she knelt beside me and drew me close to her, and I did not resist her. I put my head on her shoulder and cried as if my heart would break.

She took me up to her room and pulled off my wet boots and socks and rubbed my cold feet. Then she sat down on a chair by her window and lifted me on to her knee.

"Now tell me about it," she said.

"He's my friend," I sobbed. "Giller's my friend."

"I know," said Aunt Emma gently. "Mine, too, and you go to see him in his hut."

Surprise made me stop crying.

"How do you know?" I asked.

"Giller told me after you'd been the first time so that I wouldn't worry about where you went to. I knew you'd be safe with him."

"So that's why you've never asked me where I've been," I murmured. "You knew all the time?"

"Giller made me promise to keep your secret. We're very

old friends, Giller and I, you know."

"Yes, you said you were at school together."

"Oh, much more than that," said Aunt Emma softly. "Now tell me exactly what happened today."

As I was telling my story, we heard the crunch of wheels coming along the lane, and the ambulance lumbered past the house on its way to the river.

Aunt Emma hurried downstairs and I followed her. She ran out to ask the ambulance men if there was anything she could do to help. They told her there was nothing, but she said she would follow them along the lane. I begged so hard to be allowed to come, too, that she let me, and we hurried after the ambulance.

Its wheels scrunched through the shallow water and out on the other side. Then two men jumped out of the ambulance and set off rapidly up the hill carrying a stretcher and blankets. Aunt Emma and I crossed by the stepping stones and waited while the driver turned the ambulance around, ready for the return trip. He invited us inside to sit beside him while we waited and Aunt Emma kept my hand in hers while she talked to him. But I kept a watch on the hill behind, waiting for them to bring Giller down.

It wasn't long before I saw them, the doctor was with them. Two men carried the stretcher, and Waterloo led the little procession.

It didn't take them long to get down the hill. Giller was not a heavy man. When Aunt Emma and I went round to the back of the ambulance to see him lifted in, his eyes were still closed and his face was like carved stone. The ambulance started off and the doctor with a shake of his head to Aunt Emma followed them in his car down the valley to the hospital, while we went home.

I never saw Giller again. He died that night.

Aunt Emma grieved quietly, making no fuss, and although she tried to comfort me, I just wanted to be left alone. I was desolate, silent with grief.

"What an unnatural child she is," Cousin Jessica remarked. "After all, she found him. You'd expect her to make some fuss, wouldn't you?"

"*I* wouldn't," said Aunt Emma shortly.

I spent most of the first few days in my room playing with the treasures Giller had given me, holding them in my hands, thinking about him, remembering things he had said to me. And when I put the squirrel back inside the chest and turned the key, I felt as if I were locking away for safe keeping all that Giller had told me, important things I must never forget.

Aunt Emma and I climbed the hill and brought Selina down to our garden where she was now to live. No one spoke to me about Giller for no one knew about our friendship—no one except Aunt Emma, and she kept my secret. Perhaps because of this secret and the shared grief of Giller's death, Aunt Emma and I grew closer together. I got to know and trust her and then we were able to talk about him. Somehow I had to get used to being without him. I missed him terribly. I had counted on him and now he was gone. Even Giller had failed me, though it wasn't his fault. It was better to trust nobody, to love nobody, and then one could not be hurt. Yet I had to admit to myself that I had grown fond of Aunt Emma, and of Waterloo.

Soon a letter came from my father telling us that he and Bergit had found a house in Surrey, not too far from London. Once they had settled into it they would come and fetch me, perhaps in time for the summer holidays. "It's a charming house called 'Watermeads Cottage,'" Bergit wrote. "I think Merrie will like it as much as we do."

However, it was nearly the end of August before Bergit and my father came for me. At first I did not want to leave Aunt Emma, but I was secretly so pleased to see Bergit again that after a few days visit I was quite ready to go with her to her new home.

Part II
Bergit's House

9

My father and Bergit had been clever in finding an unusual house tucked away out of sight, hidden in deep country, yet only a mile down a muddy lane from the main road and the village. I had never seen a house quite like it. Although it was called Watermeads Cottage and belonged to my father, I always thought of it as "Bergit's house."

It was an old house, tall and thin, of whitewashed stone crossed by great dark beams. It was quite small with little windows and thick walls and had a steeply sloping roof crowned with strange knobbly chimneys. The garden, too, was small and sunny with a gay border of flowers like a wreath round the house, and there were some shady apple trees. The lane from the main road ran down to the house, but no further. Beyond the lane, a footpath led down the hill, past a barn and a boat house, which stood on an "S" shaped piece of water. This small dark lake was known as the mere, and the footpath ran on round the edge of it till it came to a lane on the other side, which led to Holt's Farm. Bergit gave me a little room of my own, next to hers and my father's. From my window I could look down onto the mere and up the other side of it to a fringe of great beech trees on the sky line, and beyond them, to the open downs.

It was all very different from Aunt Emma's country. I missed the wildness of the open fells and the hills. The pretty countryside of Surrey, with its gentle downs, filled me with restlessness. I longed for the starkness of Giller's hut in the mists of the quarry.

I felt lost at first without Aunt Emma. She had the strength of a sturdy tree whose roots went deep, a tree that had sheltered me for two difficult years.

But I came to like Bergit's house. Bergit had taken a great deal of trouble to make it attractive, and she was proud of it. The day after we arrived, she took me all over it, showing me everything. It was quite different from Aunt Emma's house, more casual and gay. Its plain modern furniture, its pictures and brightly colored curtains made Aunt Emma's house seem dingy and old-fashioned.

I liked her way of doing things, and living with her was fun. Bergit herself was even nicer than I had hoped, and so lovely to look at. I tried very hard to please her and to make her like me.

During the first week my father had to stay in London for two or three days, and school had not yet begun, so Bergit and I were alone together. I had all her attention and love, and I thrived on it.

I helped her in the kitchen and in the house and garden and she took me shopping to buy a school coat and a skirt and some warm jerseys. "I will knit one for you in the style

of my country if you would like," she offered, and I said I
would like. She took me to see the school and to meet my
teacher, and we explored some of the country near the
house.

While my father was away, Bergit and I got on happily.
But then he came home and everything was spoiled. They
were so close, so happy with one another that I felt shut out
and of no importance. I became so nervous and clumsy that
I dropped things or spilled them accidentally. One day when
I had knocked over my milk at supper by mistake, my father
made a great fuss and seemed so annoyed that I did it again,
deliberately, and it went all over the table. "No more supper for you!" he shouted, giving me a good slap, and he carried me screaming up to my room and dumped me on my
bed. I was angry with him but also pleased that I had made
him pay me some attention. After that, however good and
happy I was with Bergit, the moment he entered the house
my mood changed and I was troublesome. Bergit was
trapped between us, she loved both of us, and I stirred up
trouble between them, irritating and pricking them whenever I could. I became what in Aunt Emma's house Bergit
had once called me, "a little dark thorn."

Then school started and for a time I had new events to
think about. Things at home became a little easier, or perhaps it was just that school was the more difficult. Part of
this was because Bergit and I were looked upon as foreign-
ers, she because of her accent and I because of my brown
skin, although my father was as English as anyone in the
village.

The first day at school, I knew I would be stared at and
pushed about. I was ready to fight. Gom was in my pocket
and grasping it gave me courage. But I did not forget my
promise to Aunt Emma not to hurt anyone with it.

I was smaller than the other children in my class, so I scowled at everyone to show that I was not afraid. On the first morning when we went into the playground and the teasing started, the biggest girl of all came and stood beside me, solid and smiling. A great bolster of a girl she was, slow and good-natured and very strong. Her bulk inspired respect. She became my protector, and when she was with me, the other children left me alone. Her name was Gossie Holt, she was nine years old, and she belonged to our class because she was considered slow, if not backward. At first I only used her as my shield, but soon a kind of friendship developed between us, and I was glad when I discovered that her home was at Holt's Farm further down the lane from Bergit's house.

Gossie was really fond of me from the start. Life was more exciting for her when I was around. I had good ideas for games and thought of exciting things to do. There were a lot of things about Gossie that I did not like, her clumsy movements and the slowness of her wits maddened me. Yet often she surprised me with a delicacy and sensitivity I did not expect in her. We soon became fast friends.

On fine days she and I walked home from school together, but often in the winter Bergit fetched us in the car.

Gossie was a much loved only daughter, her brother Jimmy seven years older and almost grown up. Because I was Gossie's friend, I was always welcome at the farm. Like every farmer's wife, Mrs. Holt was endlessly busy, and I think it was a relief to her that Gossie had someone near her own age to play with, and she encouraged me to come.

Sometimes I got so mad with Gossie that I lost my temper with her. "Don't pretend to be stupider than you are," I screamed, stamping my foot at her and battering her with my fists. And Gossie, who could have flattened me with one blow, never lifted a finger against me. In fact the nastier I was to her, the more slavish she became.

Yet as I grew fond of Gossie, I discovered how nice it was to have a friend of my own age. We spent a lot of our time playing at Holt's Farm. Even when the weather was wet, there was always a barn or a loft where we could play under cover. Bergit encouraged me to go there, especially on weekends when my father was at home. It was a good way of keeping the peace between us.

For a time everything seemed to be going better. I felt happier and more settled inside myself and I suppose I was easier to live with.

Perhaps I expected too much, perhaps I had lowered my guard too soon; at any rate when the next blow fell, it set me right back again.

It was a Saturday and my father decided to unpack a case of the belongings he had brought home from Malaya and to find places for them in Bergit's house. I asked if I could help, too. He and Bergit worked hard removing the packing and paper, and dusting or washing each thing. There was a carved wooden lamp with a silk shade, several little china bowls and spoons to match, one or two ornaments of ivory, a pretty Chinese teapot, and a picture or two. I remembered seeing most of them in my father's bungalow in Malaya.

I was sweeping up some of the packing from the floor when I stopped to watch what my father was unwrapping next. Slowly the paper came off, and I held my breath with surprise and delight. In his hand he held a little water buffalo made of jade. I knew it very well. It had belonged to my mother and to my mother's mother. It was very precious, very rare and most beautiful.

"Give it to me," I begged, "let me hold it, *please*."

"Let her hold it, Robert," said Bergit, "she won't harm it." I took the little jade and held it close to me fondling it, feeling it cool and smooth against my cheek.

It was a gray-green color, the color of the rubber trees in the early morning. I knew every detail of its smooth shape, so often had I handled it as a small child.

It had been given to my mother's grandfather by a Chinese friend whose life he had saved. It was treasured and treated with reverence by the whole family, a precious and honored possession, jealously guarded, proudly displayed on ceremonial occasions in my grandmother's house. What on earth was it doing in England? Had my father taken it? What right had *he* to have it?

A great wave of homesickness swamped me, a desperate longing to be back again in Malaya where I belonged. I clutched the little jade to my heart.

"It's mine!" I shouted. "It belonged to my mother. It's mine, *mine*."

"Your mother gave it to *me*, Merrie," my father said angrily. "Give it back."

His tone was like a gust of wind to a smoldering fire; rage blazed up in me.

"I won't I won't! Why should you have it? You care nothing for my mother," I screamed at him.

Bergit came over to me then and said firmly, "Let me have it, Merrie. Look, I'll put it on the mantelpiece and then we can all enjoy it. It is such a beautiful thing it should be seen."

"Don't interfere, Bergit," said my father sharply, turning on her, "it has nothing to do with you."

Bergit looked shattered. "Robert," she exclaimed, "how *can* you speak to me like that!"

I hated to see Bergit hurt. My rage against my father redoubled.

Without a word I handed the little jade to Bergit, then like a wildcat I turned on my father. I kicked, I bit, I scratched, spitting out my hate and fury. But he quickly pinioned my arms and carried me fighting from the room. He flung me on to my bed and locked the door behind him.

I ran to the window to climb out and escape, but the drop to the ground was too much for my common sense. In any case who could I run to?

Below me I heard angry voices, Bergit and my father quarrelling over me. It gave me a certain satisfaction but at the same time I was sorry to have distressed Bergit.

Presently she came up the stairs and unlocked the door. She had brought me my tea. She sat down on my bed and put her arms round me.

"Try to stop fighting, Merrie," she said, "it doesn't do any good. You only make yourself and everyone else miserable."

For a moment I clung to her, nestling against her, enjoying the warmth and softness of her body, then I drew back.

"You're good," I said, "but my father isn't. He's bad and cruel and I hate him."

"You're wrong, Merrie, he's none of those things. He wants to be friends if only you'd let him. Won't you try?"

I thought about it for a moment, and then I shook my head. "It wouldn't work," I said.

"At least try not to fight with him, try not to irritate and upset him," she begged.

"All right," I agreed, and I made up my mind to keep out of his way.

When I went downstairs, my father had gone out to the pub and Bergit was cooking supper. The little jade water buffalo stood in a place of honor on the mantelpiece.

After that I went more often to Holt's Farm when my father was at home. During the week while he was in London, Bergit and I were happy together. I had all her attention and I blossomed in the warmth of her affection. I was pleased I did not have to share her with my father. Bergit contrived that when my father got home in the evenings I was ready for bed and having my supper, so that we did not see much of one another. I kept out of his way for her sake.

Sometimes on a weekend if I was not at the farm I spent half the day playing in my room, having first pushed a chair under the door handle in case my father surprised me by trying to come in. Safe in there, I would take my treasures out of their hiding place and play with them—Giller's little painted chest and the carved squirrel, my snake bag with Bergit's first letter to me still inside, and the few ornaments and trinkets I had brought with me from Malaya, even my old teddy bear. From my drawer I would take the clothes I had worn before I came to England, the trousers and little jacket and spread them out before me. I could not get into them any more; I had begun to grow at last. I would take the jade water buffalo from the sitting room mantelpiece and smuggle him up to my room. Holding him in my hands, I would stroke his cool smooth flank and sit daydreaming till a kind of peace came to me and I forgot my troubles for a time.

10

OUR FIRST WINTER IN BERGIT'S HOUSE PASSED QUICKLY AND without too many disturbances. Every day when I got back from school Bergit and I had time to ourselves, time to enjoy one another. We made a big fire in the sitting room and were happy together. Sometimes she read to me, sometimes we listened to the radio. She taught me to knit and to sew, and I found I learned easily and she praised my work. It was cozy in Bergit's house when we had shut out the darkness. Although the wind moaned round the chimneys and whipped up the black water of the mere, I felt secure and safe inside its strong walls. I was content to stay indoors.

Then when the spring came, I began to play outside again. Flowers were pushing green points through the borders by the apple trees, and Bergit gave me a little garden of my own where I sowed many flowers. The companionable calling of the Holt's sheep to their lambs echoed through the valley, and I began to look for new places for games.

I remembered the old barn down near the boat house on the mere.

I had never liked the mere, its face was sinister, its dark heart treacherous. Instinctively I always hurried past it, there was nothing to encourage me to loiter on its reedy banks.

When I had first come to live at Watermeads my father had taken me into the boat house. It was a dismal place, its roof moldering, its sides warped and its rotting boat rocking gently on the lapping water.

"You are not allowed to go into the boat house or to play by the mere, *ever*," said my father. "It is dangerous and I forbid it. Do you understand?"

"I don't want to play there," I retorted.

"That's not the point. Do you promise to do as I say?" he asked sternly.

"I suppose so. Yes," I had said.

I had no intention of playing near the mere, not because of obeying my father but because I was afraid of it. The mere itself, the rotting boat, the decaying boat house all induced in me a feeling of intense dislike, of revulsion, which I could not explain. In any case, the boat house was kept locked; it would not have been easy to get into it even if I had wanted to.

The barn by the boat house, however, across the path from the mere, was in good condition and looked promising as a place to play. Behind it was a steep bank, which struggled up to the pig field and the shelters full of enchanting squealing piglets.

But the place disappointed us. Although we tried it out once or twice, we preferred Gossie's barns at the farm, which were well away from the water.

Down the stream below the mere, but within sight of the house, I discovered a little sandy beach where I loved to go. The stream gurgled happily, and on the grass above it there was a great log on which I could climb or ride. No one else came to this place, it was my own special province. I did not bring Gossie there, not even Bergit. A curve of the bank hid the dark face of the mere from me, and I was able to forget it. The game I played there was a private secret game; I conjured up an invisible world of my own, and I escaped into it with absorbed delight. Sometimes I pretended that Giller came to me there and brought Selina, and we talked and laughed together. Sometimes it was in my grandmother's village I played, with my mother and her cousins and aunts and uncles. When I could, I brought the jade water buffalo with me to share in my fantasies and make them seem more real. I never brought my father into those games, nor the bungalow where we had lived with him— the *Tuan*. I preferred to forget that we had been happy with him in Malaya, my mother and I. I remembered only the damage he had done by parting me so treacherously from my mother and everyone I loved.

Watermeads was a lovely place in the spring and summer. When the sky was blue and the sun shone, even the mere looked smiling and harmless so that I lost a little of my strange fear of it—but never for long. It threatened me like a crouching beast waiting to spring; I could not rid myself of a sense of foreboding.

Yet I seldom thought of it. When school was over for the day, Gossie and I walked home together down the lane to our house, and sometimes I went on to the farm for tea, or Bergit asked her to stay for tea with us, out under the apple trees.

There were other delights. The packets of seeds I had sown in my garden had done very well. It was in a sheltered spot, and the little plot was a mass of flowers. I worked in it every day to keep it neat and free of weeds. Once Bergit bought me a tiny rose bush with miniature roses, buds the size of my fingernail. Sometimes I took a posy from my garden to my teacher at school or to Gossie's mother when I went to tea at the farm. But the best of my flowers I gave to Bergit.

The happiest time of the day for me was when Bergit and I were alone in the garden, for then she would talk to me while she sewed, telling me about her father and mother and her home in Norway; about the farm where they lived on the hillside high above the fjord whose waters changed color a dozen times a day. From the way she spoke I realized that Bergit was sometimes lonely and homesick, too.

"Speak Norwegian," I begged her. "Teach me some words." This was how I started to learn her language, and soon, if she spoke slowly, I was able to understand what she said to me, and even to answer her a little, although it was a long time before I became fluent. Although Bergit was delighted to have someone to talk to in her own language, we were careful to speak it only when we were alone together, never when my father was there. It made a bond between Bergit and me in which he had no part, and he wouldn't have liked it at all.

One day a letter came from Aunt Emma asking us all to stay with her for part of the summer holidays. I was excited and pleased, and although I knew it would not be the same for me without Giller, I began to look forward to seeing Aunt Emma again and the people I knew in the village— even that old pussy cat Cousin Jessica—and dear Waterloo.

We went up to Cumberland by car as soon as school finished. My father had arranged his two weeks' holiday at that time.

It was nice to be back in Aunt Emma's house again; the village and everything seemed much the same as when I left and yet quite different since Giller was no longer there. Waterloo's joy was overwhelming, he knocked me over and would not let me out of his sight, the darling dog! But Aunt Emma worried me, she was changed—as if something vital in her was dimmed. Not only did she look older and a little frail, something had faded and gone, something much deeper than looks. Often when we were alone she talked about Giller, remembering things they had enjoyed together, happy times they had shared, and I began to understand what he had meant to her. It was his death that had changed and broken her—she must have loved him very much. How dense I must have been not to have seen it sooner. And that time in the kitchen when Cousin Jessica, discussing Giller with Mrs. Robinson, had said, "Just as well *she* never married him. He'd have been no good to her"—it was Aunt Emma she had meant. Why had I never guessed? What had gone wrong, I wondered? What had stopped them from getting married and being happy together? Now it was too late and she was left without him, a sad old woman.

Cousin Jessica had not changed. I usually knew what she would say or do. She was as stupid as ever.

I climbed the hill to the quarry once only, and Waterloo came with me, but the desolation of the place was more than I could bear. Giller's hut was partly fallen in, his garden overrun, the mist and the wind had taken over his domain.

I slipped quite easily back into the niche I had made for myself in the village. My friends had not forgotten me and seemed pleased to see me again—even Sammy Green kept asking me to play on the village ground. I was surprised and pleased and felt more friendly towards everyone.

One day Aunt Emma asked me about Bergit. "Do you get on well with her? Are you happy living with her and your father?"

"Oh yes, I *love* Bergit, just as you said I would," I cried. "She's teaching me to speak Norwegian." I went on to tell her about Gossie and school, and I described Bergit's house to her, and the garden.

"I have my own little garden now," I said, "and I grow some really beautiful flowers. You know how much I love flowers."

"Yes, I remember," said Aunt Emma. "I am very glad that you have a settled home at last. So everything is all right, is it dearie?"

"Ye-es," I said hesitating, "only—." How could I make her understand that my father spoiled everything?

"Only? You and Robert still don't get on? You haven't forgiven him for bringing you to England. Is that it?"

I nodded my head. "He had to bring you—you're his child. How could he leave you behind?" said Aunt Emma angrily.

"I am my mother's child, too. He left her behind," I shouted back at her. "He only did it to please you, not because he wanted me."

"It was the *right* thing to do," Aunt Emma affirmed. "You have a better chance in life over here."

She did not say any more to me then but that night I was wakened by the murmur of voices by my bed. It was my father and Aunt Emma. They thought I was fast asleep, so I lay quite still.

"She's still very resentful, poor little thing," whispered

Aunt Emma. "I hoped she'd have settled down by now. Bergit is very good to her."

"She doesn't want to settle. I should never have brought her home, but you insisted. I should not have listened to you, or her mother. I should have left her behind."

"You *had* to bring her home with you, Robert, she is your child, your responsibility. She'll have a much better chance of a good life here than in a jungle village in Malaya. You *know* you did the right thing," said Aunt Emma.

"Did I? I often wonder," said my father bitterly. "I don't really want her. She is an irritation, a constant reminder of a part of my life I want to forget. Bergit was right to call her a little dark thorn, it's just what she is. I hoped everything would be better after Bergit and I were married, but the child tries to make trouble between us, she destroys my peace of mind."

"You must try to be patient, Robert, and more understanding. Perhaps when you and Bergit have a child of your own life will be easier for Merrie. She is devoted to Bergit because she knows that Bergit loves her. Can't you show her a little love, Robert?"

"What's the use," said my father, "she won't accept it. It's an impossible situation."

They went away at last and left me alone in the dark.

11

When my father's holiday was over, Aunt Emma invited me to stay on with her for a bit longer, and as Bergit
didn't mind and I knew my father would be pleased to get
rid of me for a little, I was glad to stay.

The valley was full of summer visitors, the roads busy
with cars, and Aunt Emma told me not to wander alone too
far from the house now that Bergit and my father were
gone.

"See that Waterloo goes with you," she said. "There are
some queer looking folk around nowadays in the summer."

I spent a lot of my time on the Robinson's farm. John
Stone was home and had brought a school friend with him,
and the three of us played in the shallows of the river, building dams and piers and harbors filled with paper boats.

Although I missed Bergit and looked forward to being at
home with her again, I enjoyed staying on my own with

Aunt Emma. I was very fond of her. Even Cousin Jessica seemed pleased with me and did not find fault with me so often.

"This one has improved a lot I must say," Cousin Jessica remarked to Aunt Emma at tea one day, and she nodded approvingly at me. "She's begun to look quite pretty, too."

"She always has," answered Aunt Emma, "but we do have a lot to thank Bergit for. She has made a place for Merrie."

It was true, Bergit had made a place for me, a sheltered spot where I could grow. I was learning to hide my thorns, to be more friendly, more trusting to the world in general, as my confidence grew.

Then something happened that shocked and frightened me very much.

Waterloo and I had gone to the farm higher up the valley for eggs, because the Robinsons were short and had sold out. On the way back the road was so busy with visitors' cars that I decided to cross the river and go back by the path on the other side, through the woods to the back of the village and the stepping stones at the end of our lane. We crossed by a little foot bridge and turned into the woods. It was very silent there after the noisy road, and I began to sing aloud as I walked along through the trees by the river. After a while, the egg basket seemed to grow heavier—perhaps I had made a mistake in taking the longer way home, but it was too far to go back, I'd just have to go on.

Suddenly I realized that Waterloo was no longer with me! I called and whistled—a new accomplishment I had learned only that summer—but he did not come. I was sure he had followed me over the foot bridge. Could he have turned and gone back to the farm again? I hoped he was all right—the traffic on the road was pretty fast, and it was not like Waterloo to desert me.

I had to put down the basket to have a little rest, and when I stooped to pick it up again a sudden flicker of sunlight drew my attention to one of the trees behind me, and a shadow that moved—a man was hiding there. My heart gave a little jump but I pretended not to have noticed him. I picked up my basket and walked on, a bit faster than before—Waterloo must surely appear at any moment. But when I looked round again the man was nearer, he was certainly following me, dodging half-hidden from one tree to the next. When I stopped, he stopped. There was something furtive about him that made me shudder, and as I realized that there were no houses near, I began to feel frightened and started to run.

He came on faster then, and as I ran harder, I began to wonder how much longer my legs would last. It was still some distance to the village and safety, and my breath was coming in painful gasps. I dropped my basket for I needed all my strength to escape. I prayed for someone, some hiker or visitor, *anyone* to appear on the path, or Waterloo to come bounding after me—but there was no one. I was all alone. I was getting exhausted and beginning to stumble a little so that I was afraid of falling. The village was still far away, I would never reach it before he caught me. He was gaining on me every moment, and I was becoming slower.

Desperate with fright, I took the only way of escape left to me. I ran off the path, jumped down the bank and plunged into the river.

It was lucky I landed in water only up to my armpits, not in one of the deep pools, for I could not swim. The river was low from lack of rain and flowing slowly so it did not sweep me away. The shock of the cold water compelled me to get out quickly. I struggled across to the other side, up the

bank through thorns and nettles and brambles, on to the
road, and the safety of the passing cars. I looked back across
the river half expecting to see the man following me, but
there was not a sign of him. Then my heart gave a great
bound of relief as I saw swimming across the river behind
me—Waterloo! I waited for him at the top of the bank,
and as he struggled up, his coat dripping water, I threw my
arms round him, buried my face in his wet fur and sobbed
out, "Darling, *darling* Waterloo! You're the best dog in all
the world!"

He gave himself a good shake and licked my face and
made a fuss over me as if he were apologizing for running off
for a while.

I gripped a handful of the fur on his neck and we hurried
back to the village on the grass verge of the road, while the
cars whizzed by. We must have looked a sorry couple, we
were both sopping wet, and my legs and arms were blotched
and scratched where the nettles and thorns had got me, but
I didn't care—I was safe!

Aunt Emma saw us as we walked in at the garden gate.

"Merrie! Child!" she cried. "What has happened?
Where *have* you been? And Waterloo? Did you both fall
into the river?"

Cousin Jessica dropped her gardening tool and came hurrying across the lawn.

"What's to do?" she said. "Good heavens, child! Your
arms and legs are bleeding! Poor pet, how did you hurt
yourself?"

Their concern and sympathy was too much for me, and I
must have been more shaken than I realized for suddenly
my knees gave way, and I was kneeling on the grass in Aunt
Emma's arms, sobbing.

"There, there dearie," she said. "Come along into the

house and tell us all about it."

Aunt Emma took one hand and Cousin Jessica the other and they led me into the sunny kitchen, where Aunt Emma took me on her knee and Cousin Jessica got me a drink and began to sponge my arms and legs. Waterloo sprawled close beside us and for once nobody minded what a muddy mess he was making on the clean floor.

I told Aunt Emma everything that had happened while Cousin Jessica clucked to and fro like an old hen.

"Perhaps it was just someone playing a silly joke," she suggested.

"A funny sort of joke to scare a little girl half out of her wits!" cried Aunt Emma. "And you might have been drowned, dearie, if you'd jumped into one of the *deep* pools! As for you, Waterloo," she said in a stern voice turning towards him, "why did you leave Merrie alone? What were you thinking of?"

He hung his head and looked so guilty and ashamed while he tried to decide whether to wag his tail or not, that we all began to laugh and he knew he was forgiven.

"I'm sure it wasn't a joke," I said in answer to Cousin Jessica's remark. "The man was chasing me, wanting to get *hold* of me; that's why I was so terrified."

"He must be mad," whispered Cousin Jessica.

But Aunt Emma asked, "Did you see his face? Would you know him again?"

I shook my head. At first he had been too far behind me and as he got nearer I was too intent on getting away to dare to look back at him.

"There's no one in the village would do a thing like that," said Cousin Jessica. "He must have been a visitor."

"Just the same, I'm going along to see Bob Rook to tell him about it," said Aunt Emma. Bob was the village policeman. "He must try to catch the man before it's too late."

Too late for what, I wondered? What would he have done to me if he had caught me? My mind switched away from the thought, better not to think about it.

Bob Rook came and asked a lot of questions, which I answered as well as I could.

"I'll keep a watch round the village, especially in the woods," he assured Aunt Emma, "but it's difficult with visitors. They come and go too quickly."

"Now, you forget all about it, missie," he said kindly, turning to me, "and keep that dog beside you wherever you go. Better put him on a lead, Miss Eskin," he advised Aunt Emma. "You can't be too careful."

I never heard whether they caught the man or not, and I tried to forget the whole thing, but for the few days left of my holiday I stayed in Aunt Emma's garden.

After I got home again, I talked to Bergit about it.

"I've never been so terrified in all my life," I told her. "I was afraid he was going to catch me—what would he have done to me if he had?"

"He might have done nothing at all," said Bergit, "or he might have hurt you, even killed you."

"But *why?*" I persisted.

"Because such people are sick, sick in their minds, a little mad and often dangerous. This is why I have warned you not to talk to strangers and *never* to take a lift in anyone's car unless you know them."

"What will happen to the man if they catch him?" I asked.

"He'll be persuaded to go into the hospital for treatment till he is better," said Bergit. "Now forget all about it," she advised. "It's all over and done with. There are not many people like that in the world, most people are good and friendly and kind. Let's go and pick some apples to make a pie, shall we?"

I took her hand, and we ran off together to the orchard.

But although I pushed the whole thing to the back of my mind, I could not forget it. For some time afterwards I suffered from nightmares, and I was afraid to go out alone.

Bergit did not say any more about it, but she must have understood very well what a shock it had been to me, and how nervous it had made me, for she did just the right thing.

"We're going to the nearest R.S.P.C.A. home this morning," she announced cheerfully a day later. "We're going to choose a dog for you—not a puppy, but a young dog with some sense who'll be a good friend to you."

"Oh! Bergit!" I exclaimed delightedly. "You have such wonderful ideas!"

The R.S.P.C.A. home was a grim looking building in a back street of the nearest town. Bergit explained to me that this society—its full name was the Royal Society for the Prevention of Cruelty to Animals—took in and cared for animals that were lost or had been ill-treated, till new homes were found for them.

We were taken to a yard at the back of the house where there was a collection of cages. We walked round them looking in at the dogs—dogs of all kinds and sizes and conditions, many of them thin and miserable looking, some of them cowed and beaten, all of them unwanted, unloved. It made me very angry that people could behave so cruelly to animals. "I'd like to take *all* the dogs home with me," I said.

Bergit smiled. "Only one Merrie, which is it to be? You must choose," she said.

I pointed to a cage half way down the line. I knew the dog I wanted.

He was led out into the yard and came slowly towards us,

as if uncertain of his welcome.

"That's Boris—his name was on his collar," said the kennel girl. "He's a very nice dog. We were sure someone would come to claim him, but we've had him for several weeks now and no one has."

When I held out my hand to him, he came to me quickly without fear. He had a peculiar little lift of his lip that made him look as if he were smiling. He was middle-sized and honey-colored; quite a young dog. He stood looking up at me hopefully, trustingly, and I put my hand on his head and patted him. Thanks to Waterloo, I was not frightened of dogs any more.

"Boris," I said, "you're my dog now, you belong to me. Come along. Let's go home."

Obediently, trustingly, he followed me to the car—*my* dog, Boris.

12

AFTER BORIS CAME, LIFE WENT ON MUCH AS IT HAD BEFORE, except that now there was a dog to love me and for me to love in return. Nothing else changed, and nothing notable happened until the next summer. In those summer holidays, just before my tenth birthday a wonderful thing happened—Bergit took me to stay at her home in Norway. My father came with us, but when his two weeks of holiday were over and he went back to England, Bergit and I stayed on. I was overjoyed.

It was a very happy time for me and for Bergit, too. She had seemed depressed and listless during the winter, so I understood perfectly what she meant when she said she needed to go home to her mother for a while.

The farm where she lived was even lovelier than she had described it on its hill high above the fjord. Her mother and father, Tante Helga and Onkel Lars, welcomed me as if I had been Bergit's own child, and while I was in their home

I was so happy that I even found it easy to be nice to my father. He and Bergit spent some days walking in the mountains alone together, or sailing on the fjord, and I did not mind a bit, for there were children living close to the farm in the village and round the sawmill for me to play with, and I spoke their language well enough to be understood. I liked to help feed the animals on our farm and on the next farm, the Petersens', and to ride the cream-colored ponies that worked in the fields.

Everyone was busy cutting the hay and hanging it over long lines of wire to dry in the sun, for summer came late in those high northern valleys. Sometimes Tante Helga took me to market in the town at the end of the fjord, only six miles away, or I watched Onkel Lars stacking the huge neat piles of wood for next winter's fires; there was always something interesting to do. Sometimes I visited the Petersen farm—Nils Petersen was a close friend and neighbor of Onkel Lars. There I met the two Petersen sons, Erik and Anders, and some of their friends. Anders was about my own age, but big for his years, and liked to spend his school holidays working on the farm with his father. Erik, his older brother, was a student at agricultural college, and he and his pretty fiancée Inga also worked on the farm in their summer vacation. Some day it would belong to Erik, then he and Inga would get married. Fru Petersen was dead, and old Margit looked after the house and cooked for the boys and their father.

The one thing I missed was Boris, but he had gone to live at Gossie's farm while we were away, and I knew he would be well cared for there.

On the slope of the hill close to the farm there was a tiny shack, an old one-room house where a farm worker must once have lived. It was made of wood, and it had a roof of grass turf out of which grew a tiny birch tree and a lot of buttercups and daisies. I was fascinated with this little house, especially the roof, and I asked Tante Helga if I could play in it.

"Of course you can," she said, "though you'll find there's a hole or two in the roof, and on a wet day, the rain pours through. It's years since anyone lived there, but when Onkel Lars was a boy, it was the home of the old woman who looked after the goats on the farm."

"I love the tree and flowers growing on its roof," I exclaimed.

"All the old houses here in the country used to have roofs like that once," Tante Helga said.

I invited three of the little girls I often played with into the grass-roofed house with me. I was the mother, and they all had to do what I said. We piled dry hay in one corner to sit on, and between us we collected a few old pots and pans and some chipped and cracked china and we built a stove of stones. There, absorbed and satisfied, we played games of keeping house through the long summer days. It reminded me of Giller's hut in the old quarry, it had the same quality of quietness and simplicity. He would have loved my little grass house as I did; he would have felt at home in it.

I gained a lot that summer. I felt that I really belonged to Bergit's family, that I mattered to them, that they cared what happened to me, that I was one of *them*. I wished that I could live at the farm always. Everyone was kind to me, and accepted me and I made friends wherever I went.

One day when Bergit and I had taken our lunch and climbed up the mountain behind the farm, I was able to tell her what a difference she had made to my life, and how at last I felt I really belonged to her as if I were her own child.

"Nothing must ever change that feeling, *ever*," she said to me, and her face was serious, as if she were making me a promise.

We climbed higher and higher till at last we left the path and came out into a little plateau perched above an immensely high water fall. The stream plunged in a great horsetail, out of the rock and down to the valley hundreds of feet below. The spray rose like smoke and trembled with rainbows; there was nothing but the terrible roar of the tumbling water to warn one of the sudden startling danger. It was an awesome place, beautiful and terrifying and entirely unexpected. I did not want to linger there, I was too scared, and I seized Bergit's hand and pulled her back to the path and the safety of the hillside.

All too soon the holiday was over and it was time for us to go back to England. I did not want to go.

I hated leaving Norway and the people I loved, Tante Helga and Onkel Lars, the Petersens, the children I played with and the people in the village. I was going to miss the corner I had made for myself at the farm, and I told Bergit so.

"But your father needs us, both of us," said Bergit, "and Boris—he'll have forgotten you if we don't go back soon."

The thought of Boris cheered me up, and I began to look forward to seeing him again.

When we got home, the summer was almost over and I went back to school. Boris made up to me for some of the things I had left behind; he was obviously overjoyed to be with me again. Gossie, too, was glad to have me home and we quickly settled into our winter routine. I had been so happy in Norway that now I felt more self-confident, and able to get on better with everyone, even with my father. I knew that this would please Bergit, so I was determined to try very hard with him.

On the whole we succeeded pretty well, he and I, in keeping the peace between us, but occasionally a row flared up.

The little jade water buffalo was one source of trouble. Again and again I begged my father to give it to me, I felt I needed it. But every time he refused to part with it. "Your mother gave it to *me*," he said. I could not understand why my mother should have given him something so precious to her whole family. When I asked him, he would not talk about it. She must have loved him very dearly, I supposed.

Bergit took a morning job that winter, and Mrs. Peters in the village came to clean the house. But in the holidays when I was at home, Bergit did not work and she was always there when Gossie and I got in from school.

One day when I got in for tea, Bergit, looking rather flushed and excited, met me at the door. She helped me off with my coat and pulled me into the sitting room as if she could not wait to tell me something.

"Merrie! Merrie!" she cried. "I'm going to have a baby— in the spring! I've just been to see the doctor."

"A baby?" I repeated stupidly, as if it was the most extraordinary thing I had ever heard. "Oh . . . Bergit . . . are you glad?"

"Of course I'm glad," she said laughing, "it's almost too good to be true. You must be glad, too."

"I think I am," I replied, but I felt very doubtful. How would a baby affect me? What changes would it bring? Would I feel left out in the cold?

"When the baby is born, I shall have two daughters, or perhaps a daughter and a son," said Bergit happily, and I knew it was her way of assuring me that *my* place was safe and permanent.

I thought a great deal about the baby and wished that nothing would change. I did not want to share Bergit with any newcomer. And of course the baby would be my father's, too; how would he feel about it? Would he love it as I would like him to love me? Would I be jealous of it? I chewed things over in my mind when I was alone or with Boris, but I did not want to talk to Bergit about them.

As the time of the baby's birth drew near, there was some discussion between my father and Bergit over what was to happen to me. My father wanted to send me to Aunt Emma, but Bergit wouldn't agree.

One day when I was alone with her, I suddenly burst out with, "Don't send me away when the baby is born, *please* Bergit. I'll be as good as gold and no trouble, I promise."

"But I shall have to stay in hospital for at least a week," said Bergit, looking worried. "You wouldn't be happy alone here with your father? Wouldn't you rather go to Aunt Emma, just for a little while till I am home again and strong enough to cope?"

"Oh please not," I begged. "Couldn't I stay here with Mrs. Peters? Or wouldn't she come to live in till you are back? Don't, *don't* send me away."

Bergit evidently saw that this was something that really mattered a great deal to me, and I remember very well how *much* it mattered. If I had been sent away then, I would have felt ousted by the new baby and this would have spoiled everything from the start. As it was, everything worked out very happily, for Bergit spoke to Gossie's mother, and she invited me to stay with them at the farm during Bergit's absence—it couldn't have been better.

The baby, a girl, was born at the end of May, a tiny flower of a creature, golden and white like a daisy. She was only three days old when I was allowed to visit the hospital and Bergit made me sit on her bed as she put the baby into my arms.

"She's very small," I said doubtfully. I was a little scared of her.

"Yes," said Bergit, "but healthy and she'll grow fast. We must take good care of her, Merrie."

I had not known what I would feel about the baby. I thought I might hate her, might be jealous of her. But when I held her in my arms, her face warm and soft against my cheek, I loved her at once. I was her big sister, I felt responsible for her. I would take care of her, always.

Mrs. Holt was very good to me while I stayed at the farm and Gossie was delighted to share her room with me, but I couldn't wait to get home to Bergit's house to learn to look after the baby. She was like a new toy.

Bergit allowed me to help bathe and dress the baby, to watch her being fed. It was my job to clean her pram and get it ready for her to sleep in. I hurried home from school every day so as not to miss a minute of my time with her. Gossie was forgotten for the moment, no one mattered but the baby. When she was a little older, I was allowed to push her out in her pram along the lane, and to play with her on a rug on the grass in the garden. Bergit shared her happiness in the baby with me, so that I was seldom jealous, and soon I was able to care for her almost as well as Bergit herself.

While she was very small, my father did not notice her much, he did not seem to share our joy in her; but as she grew older and learned to smile at him, he began to take an interest in her, and to show his love for her. I was glad then, for who could resist loving her. It made my father kinder and more natural, and for a time our life in Bergit's house was happier because of the baby.

She was christened Astrid Mary, but my pet name for

her, "Daisy," was the one that everyone used. It suited her best.

She was a good baby, loving and contented. She seldom cried, and I adored her.

When she was a little older, I asked to be allowed to have her in my room.

"I'll look after her," I promised. "I'll waken at once if she cries in the night."

"Perhaps we should wait till she's a year old, Merrie," said Bergit gently. "At least till she has finished cutting her first teeth."

"But I waken always when she cries," I objected, "and if she was in my room, I could soon quiet her." It was true, she would stop crying for me when even Bergit had failed to pacify her.

But surprisingly, my father objected.

"You treat her like a dolly, you pamper and spoil her already," he growled at me. "She'd be better off away from you in a room of her own."

"Oh Robert, that's unfair and unkind," cried Bergit. "Merrie is marvelous with our baby, and you know it! I can't see why you are so unreasonable."

I was hurt and angry with him and all the old hostility sprang up between us again. I turned on him in a rage, but Bergit took me by the shoulders and shook me.

"Stop it!" she said. "That's enough. You'll only frighten the baby."

I stopped at once and ran out of the room, leaving Bergit and my father glaring at one another.

But I had my way over Daisy; very soon after her first birthday she was moved into my room.

13

AFTER I WAS TWELVE I WENT TO A NEW SCHOOL, A PRIVATE school, which was partly for day girls and partly for boarders. I liked it well enough, though I did not see so much of Gossie. We no longer came home from school together. But we played together all weekend, and the two of us took Daisy out in her stroller, for Gossie was almost as enthralled with her as I was. We used to push her along the lane, or around the path by the mere to the Holts' farm with Boris proudly escorting us. I always hurried along the path by the water, fearful that something might happen—that the stroller might overturn and the baby be thrown into the mere. When there had been heavy rain and the mere was full, its waves lapped on to the path like greedy lips trying to suck us into the water, to swallow us down. There were no end to the frenzies I had about that place, and no explanation of the panic I felt.

Then early in the fall Gossie's mother became worried about her being so overweight and took her to a doctor who sent her into the hospital for treatment. When she came home again, slimmer and almost elegant, she was on a strict diet, and her parents decided to send her to a special school as a boarder for a few years. I missed her very much; she was my best friend. I was used to having her always around, and although I bossed her about shamefully, I enjoyed her good-natured company and felt quite lost without her. I would have missed her even more if I had not had Daisy to play with and care for. More and more of my time was taken up with teaching her to talk, and watching that she did not hurt herself by falling down the steep stairs, or tripping over the rough stone of the kitchen floor.

When I had been at my school for a term, a new girl arrived, a Malayan girl called Munah. She was put in my class, and I was asked to look after her. She was very miserable and homesick at first, and I, remembering how I had felt when I first came to England, did my best to cheer her up. I asked Bergit to invite her to tea one Sunday. But my father was not at all pleased when he heard about it. When Munah came, his manner to her was very correct, but cold and formal, and I was embarrassed. He did not want us to be friends, he wanted me to forget Malaya, and he did not like to be reminded of it himself. I was angry with him and made a great fuss over Munah, which annoyed him even more. But she seemed undisturbed, she was very polite. She enjoyed playing with Daisy, for she had little sisters of her own at home. I took her to my room and showed her my treasures, the things that Giller had made for me, my snakeskin bag and even Gom.

When we came downstairs again, my father had taken Daisy out, and Bergit was resting, so we went into the sitting room where Boris lay stretched out before the fire. As she stood warming herself by the fire, she suddenly gave a little cry of surprise and picked up from its place on the mantelpiece the water buffalo. "Oh how lovely," she said, "it's jade! Whose is it?"

"It belonged to my mother—now it is mine," I lied.

Munah examined the jade closely and with interest. "It is a beautiful piece," she said. "You should take great care of it. I'm sure it is worth a lot of money."

"How do you know?" I asked.

"Because my father is a collector, and in my home we have many pieces," she said. "Does it really belong to you?"

"Yes," I lied again, "it's mine."

"Tell me about your home," I asked to change the subject. "Tell me about Malaya."

So she described her family life, the fine house in the town where she lived, where her father was an official, an important man. But of the country inland, the poor villages I remembered, the jungle and the rubber plantations, she said nothing. I think she had never seen them; they did not belong to her world. I was disappointed that we did not have more in common. I had hoped that because of my Malayan mother we would have become close friends, naturally drawn to one another, but it was not so. She made me feel very English.

"Why did you come to England?" I asked. "Did you choose to come or were you sent?"

"I *chose* to come," Munah explained. "You see, I want very much when I am older to go to the Oxford University, so therefore I must come first to school in England. For you it is easy, you live here. I envy you."

It was a point of view I had not met before, and it made me think.

But I did not ask her home again, it was too uncomfortable.

The following summer, Onkel Lars and Tante Helga came from Norway to stay with us for a month. I was delighted to see them and I tried to please them, for they had been good to me when I stayed in their home. I asked them about my friends in the village, about the people who worked on their farm and in the sawmill, about the Petersens. I wanted to hear about all of them.

"Your friends have not forgotten you," Tante Helga assured me, "all of them sent their greetings. The Petersen farm is Erik's now. He and Inga are married and they have a little son. Nils Petersen had a bad heart attack and cannot work any more, but Inga is very good and looks after him with old Margit's help. Everyone hopes you'll come back again soon, Merrie."

Her words gave me a wonderful feeling of warmth, so I did not mind about the fuss she and Onkle Lars made over Daisy. She was their first real grandchild, of course, but they never let me feel left out or of less importance to them, and I loved them for that. There was not so much tension in the house during their visit; Bergit was happier because my father was better tempered, and I really tried while they were there not to annoy him.

After they had gone back, my father and Bergit invited Aunt Emma to come on a visit, but although she had never seen Daisy nor Bergit's house, they could not persuade her to come. She would not leave home, and my father went alone to Cumberland to see her in the autumn.

A wild winter followed, with great gales that shook the leaves early from the trees, and whipped the black water of the mere with foam. I was irritable and filled with a nagging anxiety, a presentiment of disaster. My phobia with the mere built up more and more. I became obsessed with the notion that an evil force, an elemental power, lay hidden in its black water. The local people were right to call it a "bad" place.

I conjured up an image of this force, which became for me the symbol of all evil in the same way as the little jade personified goodness and light.

I scared myself with my own imaginings, which soon grew beyond my control. Sometimes on a stormy night I was wakened by a tapping on my window, bony fingers demanding an entry. I knew it was only a harmless twig on the apple tree, but in the darkness I felt it might be anything. Sometimes when mist hung low, filling the valley and shrouding the house, I thought that a shape rose dripping from the mere and hung swirling outside my window, waiting to envelop me. I even gave it a name. The dru, I called it.

Once, I was certain that something had gotten into the loft above my room. There were thuds on the ceiling and bumpings against the walls, and Boris, who liked to sleep on the rug outside my door, began to growl and whine. It was probably only a bird that had flown in under the rafters to shelter for the night. When I dared to climb the ladder to the loft next morning to have a look around, nothing had been disturbed, there was no sign of occupation.

Yet the fear persisted, I could not shake off the sense of foreboding. I was haunted by a blind irrational dread.

When the spring came, my father began to make short business trips abroad, and Bergit, Daisy and I were left on our own. These were happy times; there was a wonderful relaxed feeling of freedom in the house. I *did* what I liked and *said* what I liked. Tension and restrictions disappeared while my father was away.

Bergit seemed to grow younger and lost the look of strain she often wore. It was then that I reailzed how much she had changed. In spite of having Daisy to love, and me, she was not very happy with my father. There were often sharp words and sometimes quarrels between them, and when my father was angry with me, Bergit often took my part against him and there was trouble between them. I am sure that Bergit loved him and tried to make him happy, but he was a strange uneasy person to live with, full of contradictions.

As Daisy grew older, the room she and I shared became more of a nursery for her, and although I loved having her there with me, there were times when I needed to be by myself. I had reached my teens, and I had a craving for privacy. I spoke to Bergit about it, and she suggested I could use part of the loft over my bedroom as my private haunt. There was one little window in it that looked out beyond the mere and up the valley to the Holts' farm, and the main chimney of the house came up through it so that it was always warm there. Bergit made it comfortable for me; together we carried a chair up the ladder, and I put it in the corner by the window where the floor had been boarded over. I put a plank across two flower pots to make a shelf for my books, and I spread an old sheepskin rug on the floor so that I could stretch out at full length. There was always a scent of apples in the loft, it was here they were stored all through the winter.

Underneath the window where the sloping roof met the floor, there was a little space between the rafters where the boarding came to an end. It was a splendid hiding place for my treasures—Gom, my snakeskin bag, and the things that Giller had made for me. I laid a piece of wood across the cavity, and no one would have suspected that it was not part of the flooring. From time to time I added to my store, a stone of unusual color or a strangely shaped piece of wood, even the odd polished bone I found on the hillside, left by a hunting owl.

I loved this private haunt of mine where I was undisturbed. My father never came up except to store the apples after they were picked, and Bergit only when she needed some for cooking. She respected my privacy.

When I was in trouble, I hid up there till I recovered. I played my secret game and escaped into my private world. I . borrowed the little jade and held it in my hand. It had an almost magical power to soothe me, to give me back my peace of mind. It transported me to Malaya, to my mother, to my grandmother's *kampong*, to my early years before I came to England. It was a beautiful nostalgic dream of my childhood, partly remembered but mostly embroidered by my imagination into an extravagant fantasy. The little jade became more and more precious to me. It stood for all I had loved in Malaya. It was my symbol of security, of happiness, of everything that was good and lovely.

14

Our summer holiday the year I was thirteen, almost fourteen, was to be spent at Aunt Emma's village, but this time we were not to stay in the house with her; Bergit insisted that we were too many for the two old women, so we rented a cottage close to them.

At the last minute before we left, I had a sudden impulse. While Bergit and my father were busy packing the car, I slipped into the sitting room, took the water buffalo from the mantelpiece and ran up to the loft with it. I put it into my hiding place with my other treasures—it would have company while we were away!

When I got back to the car, there was just time to say goodbye to Gossie and her mother, who had come to see us off. I jumped into the back beside Daisy while my father locked the front door of the house and gave the key to Mrs. Holt before he drove off.

It took us most of the day to reach Aunt Emma's village, and I was glad to find it unchanged. There were one or two new faces, and a few of the old ones were missing; there were several newly built houses, and a few old ones had been repaired and painted. It was a good thing we had left Boris behind with Mrs. Holt, for Waterloo, who looked on me as his special property, nearly went mad with joy at seeing me. He and Boris would have fought one another, I'm sure.

Aunt Emma looked better, but although she was less frail-looking than she had been the last time I stayed with her, she seemed to have lost her interest in us, and in everything. Her mind had closed up, so that it was difficult to talk to her. She seemed to have withdrawn into some secret retreat where I could not follow her. She was impatient with Daisy and tired of her quickly—this was not the Aunt Emma I had known and loved. The change in her distressed me, and I spoke to Bergit about her.

"She's not really *there* half the time," I said. "What has happened to her?"

"She's getting old, Merrie," Bergit tried to comfort me, but I knew it was more than old age. Cousin Jessica was getting old too, but she was the same as I remembered her, slower perhaps and just as stupid.

I was proud of Daisy and enjoyed showing her off to my friends—to Mrs. Robinson at the farm, to Gracie, who was now quite grown up and had just gotten married, and to the girls who had been at school with me. When I took her to the shop, people used to exclaim with admiration, "What a lovely little girl," or "That child looks like an angel." Daisy never noticed their remarks but I scowled at them, they ignored me altogether. I couldn't quite suppress a twinge of jealousy, but I did not blame Daisy.

There were days when Bergit and my father went off alone and I was left in charge of my little sister. We would go to Aunt Emma's house for our dinner and play in my old room or with Cousin Jessica's pussy cats in the kitchen. I took very good care of Daisy. I saw that she was clean and tidy and I would not let her out of my sight even inside the garden.

One day Aunt Emma noticed this and exclaimed quite sharply, "Leave that child alone, Merrie. She can come to no harm here. Don't stifle her, she's a *person* not a dolly."

Why had she said that? My father had once said the same thing. Can you love someone too much so that it harms them, smothers them? I knew that Daisy depended on me. She did exactly what I told her and hated to be parted from me. I only wanted to protect her, to keep her safe and happy, and how could that harm her, so what did Aunt Emma mean? Perhaps I protected her too much? Perhaps she meant that I should help Daisy to stand on her own feet, to stop relying on me? I felt a little uneasy and tried to forget what Aunt Emma had said, after all she was no longer very dependable, her moods were variable.

But I noticed that she was always at her best when she was with my father. He knew this and tried to spend some time with her every day. He was wonderfully gentle and patient with her, and always kind. He sat with her in the garden or took her out in the car, every day he gave her some little treat. I was astonished how different he was from the father I knew at home. He was like a son to her. I could see that he loved her dearly, there was a long established trust between them.

Time flew by in Aunt Emma's green valley, now drowsy with summer heat, now misty with rain. I did not visit the quarry where Giller had lived, I did not want to see again the desolation, the emptiness. I preferred to remember it as it had been when Giller was alive.

The holiday came to an end, and early one morning we left for home. It was evening when we got to Bergit's house, and Daisy was asleep with her head on my lap. Mrs. Holt came out on to our door step as soon as she heard the car. I could see by her face that something was wrong. My father jumped out and went to speak to her—then I noticed that one of the sitting room windows had been smashed. Bergit ran after my father and they hurried into the house with Mrs. Holt, but I did not want to waken Daisy, so I stayed where I was.

It seemed ages till they came out again. Mrs. Holt waved to me, but she went home without saying a word, and my father picked Daisy up in his arms and carried her in to bed. When Bergit turned to me, I saw that she had been crying.

"What is it?" I asked anxiously. "Oh, Bergit, what has happened?"

"We've had a burglary," she said. "Our lovely Danish silver is all gone and some of our nicest wedding presents, the radio and TV of course, and our best floor rug. I don't know what else yet, there hasn't been time to look."

"Oh! Bergit!" I cried distressed. "What a shame! I'm dreadfully sorry. It's awful but I'm sure the police will catch the thieves and find our things."

Bergit lifted her shoulders in a gesture of hopelessness and began to collect things from the car to take inside. I followed her example.

"When did it happen?" I asked.

"Yesterday. Mrs. Holt has been round the house every day and everything was all right. But when she came up about teatime today to switch on the water heater for us, this is what she found. They must have broken in last night."

We had just finished emptying the car when with a rush of joyful barking, Boris came bounding up from the farm. I put my arms round his neck and hugged him. I was so happy to see him again that I soon forgot about the burglary. It would never have happened if he had been in the house.

While we had a late supper just to cheer us up, we left Daisy asleep upstairs. There did not seem much point in waking her. Bergit and I washed up the dishes, then while my father went around trying to find out what else was missing to add to the list of things stolen, Bergit switched on the fire in the sitting room and went to make our coffee.

It was while we were waiting there that I saw my father look along the mantelpiece and spot the empty space where the little jade water buffalo usually stood, and I remembered that I had hidden it in the loft. I pretended not to see when he got up and looked carefully along the mantelpiece as if searching for it. He said nothing and I watched him write it down on his list of missing things, but I did not tell him that I had hidden it and it was safe.

Perhaps if he had mentioned it, or made some exclamation of distress, I would have told him, but after a minute when Bergit came in and he still said nothing, it was too late. I felt bad, wicked, and I was ashamed, but I let him think that the little jade had been stolen so that I could keep it for myself.

"I'll tell him later, some other time when all this bother is over," I told myself. I did not think of its value, and that my father might claim a large sum of money for its loss; I thought only of the pleasure I had in it, and the delight of possessing it myself.

Bergit came up with me when I went to bed, and together we undressed Daisy without wakening her and tucked her in.

"You won't be nervous, Merrie, will you?" Bergit asked. "The burglars won't come back again you know. We'll leave a light on all night, and Boris is here now."

Boris, who had followed us upstairs, pricked up his ears at his name and gave his lopsided smile.

"Darling Boris!" I cried. "No, of course I'm not nervous. I just hope all your lovely things will be found, Bergit."

She left me then, and Boris pattered down after her, to return later to sleep outside my door.

When I was ready for bed, I crept out of my room and up the ladder to the loft. I just wanted to make certain that the little jade, *my* little jade, was safe.

A huge moon shone through the window, making everything as light as day. I crossed the floor and lifted the board —my treasures were undisturbed. I took them out one by one, the water buffalo, the squirrel, Gom, and Giller's painted chest. I held the jade against my cheek, rubbing it gently up and down my face and over my mouth, enjoying its delicious coolness, its smooth beauty.

Beyond the window, the landscape lay bathed in cold light, the mere in the valley, the woods stretching up the hillside, the Holts' farm—all so beautiful they seemed unreal, exaggerated. I stared at the glittering face of the mere, a peaceful face, harmless, innocent. But I was not deceived. I knew that beneath its seeming benevolence, evil lay in waiting. I knew it in my bones, and I was afraid.

15

Munah did not come back to school after the summer. I was sorry and wondered what had happened to her. Then I had a letter from her that made me think again about what she had said once before.

"My father is sick, very sick," she wrote, "and my mother needs me at home. I am the eldest. I will not be coming back to school, I will not be going to the Oxford University. I am sad about this, but my family comes first. How lucky for you that you live in England. I envy you your opportunities. There is nothing that you cannot do there, while I must be content with what my own country offers."

It was astonishing that she who seemed to have everything, should envy me living in *England!* What were the opportunities she meant? I began to wonder if perhaps England *was* a better place for me than the Malaya of my dreams. Was it possible that my father had done the best thing for me after all?

Autumn passed into winter and I kept my secret about the little jade. Once or twice I was on the point of telling my father that I had it safely hidden, but I could not bear the thought of parting with it. No trace had been found of the things that were stolen from Bergit's house.

After Christmas, Daisy, who was now nearly four years old, began going to a play group twice a week, in preparation for starting school when she was five.

We all spoiled her a little. She was such a darling, everyone loved her.

During one of the winter storms the barn by the mere was blown down, and my father got a couple of men to come and repair it. The old boat house, which was in much worse condition, remained standing, although there were great gaps in its sides where the wood had rotted. But it was not worth repairing, it was never used anyway; there was no boat, and one day it would just quietly disintegrate into the mere.

Daisy liked the two workmen and was always begging me to take her to watch them at work. Sometimes while I was at school, Bergit would leave her with them for a short time if they promised to keep an eye on her.

Daisy had to keep the same rule my father had made for me. She was not allowed to go near the mere alone. I had never needed a rule to keep me away from the mere, it frightened me too much; but this was not true of Daisy. It seemed to have a fascination for her, and had she not been such an obedient little girl, she might often have slipped away to play there.

Soon it was April and we thought that winter was over. But gales blew up and a bitter east wind that turned the tender blossoms brown and shriveled the young leaves on the trees. The violent wind shrieked like a fury round the house, tearing the tiles off the roof, snapping trees like matchsticks, hurling great branches to the ground, whipping the mere into a frenzy, and causing havoc wherever it went. Its violence bred violence, my father and I erupted into open hostility. We swore at one another, the smoldering animosity we felt for one another burst into passionate quarrels. When Bergit tried to make peace between us, she was dragged into the battle. Only when Daisy was distressed by us did we leave off fighting.

Bergit was always trying to patch up the feud between my father and me, but our antipathy went too deep, there was not much she could do.

"Your father is a good man, a kind man," she said, "why have you built him up into such a monster in your mind? Why must there be such emnity between you? I cannot understand it. It makes life miserable for us all!"

I thought of gentle Onkel Lars. No wonder she could not understand us. If Onkel Lars were my father, how different I would be.

After one of those rows with my father I dreaded going to bed. I knew what bad dreams I would have—nightmares! They usually started off quite sensibly but then they became confused, and I found I was fighting not my father but my old enemy the mere. I was struggling with the creature of my imagination, the dru, trying to shake off its reedy hand, wrestling with its slithery coils, striving to rid myself of the suffocating tendrils that wrapped themselves round my face. Horrible—*horrible!*

When I woke in the darkness, I was trembling with fright, my body in a cold sweat. Sometimes I darted from my bed to lift the sleeping Daisy in beside me and hold her in my arms till I was calm enough to fall asleep. Sometimes

I dared not even move more than to put a groping hand under my pillow to find and hold the little jade, which I put there every night. It was my safeguard, my talisman, my protector from evil.

One night I decided I must do something, take some action to avert the disaster that threatened me—an offering, a gift to pacify, to conciliate! What had I to give? Something that I valued, something that was dear to me. It was worth trying.

In the morning I went up early to the loft, and from their hiding place I took my treasures. One by one I held each in my hand, assessing its worth, trying to decide which one to part with—and in the end I chose Gom.

Once I had made the decision, I put the others back and for a day or two I carried Gom around with me in my pocket as I had done as a small child. Gom the defender, how much I had relied on it when I was younger. It had been my symbol of strength, and although I no longer needed it, the thought of parting with it was painful, like the discarding of an old friend.

It was evening when I ran down to the mere, Daisy was in bed and asleep. It was not yet dark, but in the half light of that between-world when day merges into night, anything seemed possible.

I grasped Gom in my hand, clenching it tightly, holding it high. Then with all my strength I threw it far out into the black water. I waited for the splash, holding my breath, half hoping for some manifestation to rise from the surface, like the hand that rose to grasp the sword Excalibur in the legend of King Arthur. But there was nothing, nothing but an eerie silence. I shivered as I fled back to the house.

Later, when I was undressed and ready for bed, I opened the window and leaned out of it for a moment to listen. It was a dark night and very still. The note of the owls calling across the water had a hollow sound, an echo of doom. I closed the window, climbed into bed, and fell asleep with the little jade clutched tightly in my hand.

In the early morning, before it was light, I woke. Mocking laughter came to me from the mere—a bird call? It sounded unearthly, pitiless—I had accomplished nothing, my magic had not worked, Gom was not enough. I would have to try again. A bird call? My common sense told me it was only that, there was nothing to be afraid of. And yet . . . and yet . . .

Before I left for school, while the others were finishing breakfast, I slipped outside and hurried down to the mere. Hidden under my frock I carried my dearest treasure, the most precious thing I possessed—the little jade water buffalo. For a moment I held it against my cheek thinking of all that it stood for, all it invoked, then with a whispered entreaty I threw it into the mere.

16

I MUST TRY TO SET DOWN EXACTLY HOW IT HAPPENED, though the picture has become less vivid in my efforts to forget the whole tragedy.

It was an afternoon in July, a hot lazy day. Bergit had fetched me from school in the car to save me the journey in the stuffy bus. We drove with all the windows open and Daisy standing behind me in the back.

I had a bath and got into my bikini, and Bergit carried tea out into the garden under the apple trees. She had kept some strawberries in the shade, and they were deliciously cool. Daisy and I ate as many as we could. Boris lay sighing in the shade; he did not care for strawberries and was longing for his piece of cake when we had finished.

I helped Bergit carry the tray inside and offered to wash up but she wouldn't let me.

"You've got your homework to do," she said. "But have a

little rest in the shade first. Daisy can stay with you while I get dinner started."

I went back into the garden and lay down on the rug under the tree beside Daisy, with Boris stretched alongside.

"Will you take me down to the mere?" she begged. "I want to play beside the water."

"Not now, darling. I'm too hot," I replied. "Perhaps later. Go and get a book, and I'll read you a story if you like."

She ran in and came back with her favorite picture book, a story we both knew by heart. We lay on our stomachs side by side and Daisy turned the pages, and joined in as I read the words, slowly and more and more drowsily . . .

A twig falling on my bare shoulder woke me with a start —I must have dropped off to sleep. Daisy had gone, leaving the story book open beside me. She must have got bored, I thought, when I stopped reading, and had run in to Bergit.

I felt deliciously lazy; just a few more minutes then I must get on with my homework. I resettled myself more comfortably on the rug, but I did not go to sleep again.

Presently I got up and strolled into the kitchen. Bergit was alone at the sink.

"Where's Daisy?" I asked.

Bergit looked up. "I thought she was with you in the garden."

"I fell asleep for a few minutes, didn't she come in here?" I asked. "She's probably gone up to our room. I'll find her."

I ran upstairs calling her name, but she was not there, nor anywhere in the house.

"She can't have gone far," I said to Bergit, but I felt suddenly anxious. "I'm terribly sorry," I cried, "but honestly I thought she was with you. Perhaps she's hiding from us."

"You couldn't help falling asleep," Bergit comforted me. "She can't be far away."

We went into the garden together and called and called, "Daisy! Daisy!" But there was no answer.

"Where's Boris?" I asked. Even as I spoke, from the direction of the mere came a terrible long-drawn howl that tore the sweetness of the summer day and froze me to the ground. It was Boris.

Bergit and I shot across the lawn and raced at top speed down the path towards the water to where the good dog stood whimpering by the boat house. Bergit reached him ahead of me, and I saw her pause a moment and then jump into the mere.

The first thing I noticed was a new hole in the rotting side of the boat house, and beyond it, Bergit was swimming towards something—a little bundle of white and gold that floated on the water.

I waited for what seemed like a hundred years, not knowing what to do. Then Bergit struggled ashore with Daisy in her arms. She shouted in a high harsh voice, "Phone for the doctor! Quickly! Quickly!"

For a moment I couldn't get my legs to move, then I was running like mad for the house. I reached the telephone and dialed. In a moment, panting painfully, I gasped into it, "Dr. Morris . . . please . . . he must come."

It was Dr. Morris himself "Who is it?" he asked

"It's Merrie, Merrie Eskin! Come quickly! Daisy . . . is drowned," I cried.

"I'll come now, at once," he said. "Wait for me at the house."

I did not know what to do while I waited—what could anyone do? I lit the gas. I put a kettle on although the heat of the day was still almost overwhelming. Should I ring my father? I knew I never could tell him what had happened. He might already have left the office.

Dr. Morris arrived before I expected him; he must have driven like the wind. He jumped out of the car, and we ran down the path to the mere.

Bergit was crouched over Daisy trying to revive her, but before we reached them, Dr. Morris sent me back to the house.

"Go and make us a cup of tea, Merrie. We'll need it when we come in," he said.

I turned and went back to the house, moving in a kind of nightmare. I was glad to have something to do.

I was in the kitchen when I heard them come in and go upstairs.

I made the tea and waited. Presently Dr. Morris came down alone, and I poured him out a cup.

His face told me what I already knew. "We were too late," he said.

I stood quite still. There was nothing to say. I felt as if I were made of lead; I could not think or cry or move.

"Now, try to tell me exactly what happened," Dr. Morris said.

I had to try hard. My voice seemed to come from a long way off, but I told him the whole story.

"It was my fault," I heard myself say. "If only I hadn't fallen asleep."

"It was *nobody's* fault," Dr. Morris said firmly. "It was an accident."

"Where's Bergit?" I asked.

"I have given her a pill and made her lie down," said Dr. Morris. "You can take her up a cup of tea if you will. I am going to ring Mrs. Holt and ask her to take you to the farm for the night, then I will wait with Bergit till your father comes home."

He did not talk any more about what had happened.

When Mrs. Holt arrived, he met her at the door and spoke to her, then he called me. Mrs. Holt was very distressed; tears ran down her cheeks and she could not speak. But my tears had frozen inside me, I could not cry.

"Come then, lovey," said Mrs. Holt putting an arm round me and drying her eyes, but I pulled away from her; I was still in my bikini.

"I must get my clothes on," I protested, "and my things for the night."

"You can borrow Gossie's," said Mrs. Holt. "Anything you need. Come along."

I knew then that they had taken Daisy to our room, and they did not want me to see her.

I put on the shirt and shorts I had left in the kitchen before tea and I went quietly with Mrs. Holt. It was the easiest thing to do. I felt too weary, too shattered to argue. Boris came with me.

We had supper in the big farm kitchen, and I wished that Gossie were at home. Although the familiar homely room gave me some comfort, the floor of my world had crumbled, and I felt in danger of falling though it into nothingness.

I could not swallow much supper. I was deadly tired. While the men were still eating, kind Mrs. Holt took me up to bed and tucked me up with a motherly kiss.

"It won't seem quite so bad tomorrow, lovey," she whispered.

But next morning it was worse. Mrs. Holt wanted me to stay on with them at the farm, but I had to go home. I had to see Bergit and my father. I had to make certain that it had really happened, that it was not just a horrible nightmare. I had to see for myself that Daisy was gone. It was no use putting it off, no use pretending to myself. I must face up to the fact; Daisy was dead, and I was partly to blame.

"Shall I come with you, Merrie?" Mrs. Holt asked, but I shook my head. I wanted to go alone, without even Boris. I tied him up.

"Come back to us here as soon as you can," she said.

It was a shining beautiful morning, and the mere when I reached it was innocently blue—it should have been black as pitch. My feet carried me along the path towards the boat house. I felt like a clockwork figure moving automatically.

I had almost reached the barn when a sound coming from it stopped me. I tiptoed to the door and peeped in. My father sat hunched on the straw, his face covered by his hands, sobbing in tearing painful gasps. I had never seen a man crying before. It shocked and hurt me terribly. I wanted to run to him at once, to put my arms around him, to hold his head against me, to comfort and love him. But I could not, I did not dare to. I knew he would hate for me to see him like that, and if ever he found out that I had, he would be dreadfully angry with me. I turned and crept out of the barn. But I knew what Daisy had meant to my father. I had seen for myself his desperate grief, a grief that I shared and understood. From that moment my attitude towards him began to change, my feelings began to soften slightly.

Bergit was washing up the breakfast things when I reached the house, her face gray, rigid, her eyes dull. We did not touch one another. Although she asked me if I was all right at the farm, there was a wall between us, we could not talk. I dried the dishes, then I went upstairs to my room, but the door was locked. I took refuge in the attic in my familiar corner.

The house was very still, very empty. I could not believe

that Daisy was no longer there. It couldn't be true. She couldn't be dead. I felt at any moment I would hear her voice in the garden, her step on the stair. I thought back to yesterday. Only a few hours ago she had lain beside me under the apple tree while I read to her. How could she have vanished, so suddenly, so irrevocably. I knew I would never see her again, not in our world. But I would not believe that this was the end. Surely part of her must survive in another world unknown to us, a heaven just beyond our reach? One day I might find her again in some other child, perhaps in a child of my own.

I heard the telephone ringing and went down to answer it, but Bergit was already there and spoke briefly into it. I followed her back to the kitchen and found she had been doing some washing, perhaps it helped her to keep her hands busy.

"When can I come home?" I asked timidly.

There was no softening of her stern face and she did not look at me as she replied, "After the . . . perhaps in a day or two, we'll see." Her voice had a brittle quality, as if it hurt her to speak. I offered to hang out her washing, but she did not answer me. She seemed to be sealed off into a private impenetrable despair where I could not reach her. The change in her was frightening.

I took my forgotten homework out into the garden but I could not look at it. Too much had happened. It seemed like the end of the world, my world. Daisy was dead, Bergit a stranger who hated me, how could I go on living in Bergit's house? I was back where I had started years ago, unwanted, unloved—but this time it was myself I blamed.

17

I WENT BACK TO SCHOOL FOR THE LAST FEW DAYS OF THE term, and before they were over Gossie came home for the summer holidays. She had been in no way involved in the accident nor its aftermath, and I found I could talk to her about Daisy and cry with her. Bergit's frozen silence appalled and hurt me, but Gossie was wonderfully kind and warm. It was a great relief to me to be with her. One of Gossie's remarks comforted me a bit. "I see her face in every flower," said Gossie. I liked to think that this was true, that Daisy was really not far from me.

When school was over, I expected my father to bring me home again, and I was dreading it. Bergit's strange mood, the tragic emptiness of the house and the feeling that both of them blamed me for the accident upset me. I did not know what to do. But Mrs. Holt invited me to stay on with them for as long as I wanted, and my father accepted this for another week, then I was to go to Aunt Emma's.

It was a busy time on the farm, there were many litters of new young piglets in the sheds, and the Holts were glad of my help. But however busy we were, I always made time every day to go home for a little while to see Bergit, to try to talk to her. And every day I failed to make any contact, to break through her icy despair to the Bergit I loved, the real Bergit. Nothing I said seemed to touch her, she was indifferent to me and to everything, too broken-hearted to respond. I wondered what she was like when my father was with her, and whether he was able to comfort her. I felt terribly worried and depressed, and I did not know what to do.

At last I went up to Aunt Emma's by train. Mrs. Holt and Gossie came to see me off, and Boris went home to be with Bergit.

Dr. Stone met me and drove me up the valley to Aunt Emma's house.

"How is Aunt Emma?" I asked as we bounced along the part of the road that was like a switchback.

"You'll see a change in her, Merrie," the doctor warned me. "She is very forgetful and confused, her memory has partly gone. I don't know how much longer she'll be able to stay on in her own house."

"But Cousin Jessica's still there, isn't she?" I asked.

"Oh yes, but she's not much younger than your aunt, and I doubt whether she'll be able to manage much longer, even with help from the village." It was another shock for me.

"Does my father know about this?" I asked.

"Yes, he knows, but he has troubles enough at home at the moment, hasn't he?"

"Yes," I agreed sadly, "he has." And I thought of all that had happened to us and hoped Dr. Stone wouldn't talk about it.

"Your Aunt Emma is very fond of you, Merrie, perhaps she'll cheer up while you're with her."

"I hope so," I said.

Cousin Jessica must have been watching for us from the window for as soon as Dr. Stone's car stopped at the gate, she came waddling out to meet me, rounder and fatter than ever.

"Oh, *there* you are, dearie," she said, giving me a warm hug, which half smothered me. "I'm so glad to see you. It's kind of you to bring her, doctor. Emma will be ever so pleased. She talks about her so much."

"Thank you for meeting me," I said to Dr. Stone.

"Come and see us, Merrie, whenever you like. Johnny is at home," he said. Johnny Stone—I had forgotten his very existence!

I carried my case up the stairs to my old room while Cousin Jessica puffed along behind me. I stood in the doorway looking round me with pleasure, nothing in it had changed since I was a little girl, only last time I had been here, Daisy was with me. A sob gathered and forced itself up painfully so that when I spoke to Cousin Jessica, it came out in a sort of tearless gasp.

"Where is Aunt Emma?" I asked.

"In her room. I'll take you to her when you've had a wash," Cousin Jessica said. "She's having a little snooze. I expect she's forgotten you are coming. Don't be surprised if she doesn't remember you at first, dearie, her memory is very bad and she gets confused, you know. Call me when you're ready." Aunt Emma mightn't remember *me?* Whatever could have happened to her?

Cousin Jessica hurried off down to the kitchen as the smell of supper came drifting up the stairs.

I unpacked my belongings and hung my dresses in the cupboard. After I had had a good wash in the lovely soft brown water, I put on a clean shirt and a pair of jeans. I wanted to go into Aunt Emma's room by myself, but I did not wish to make trouble with Cousin Jessica as soon as I arrived. I called her as she had asked me to do.

She threw open the door of Aunt Emma's room and said loudly to the small figure sitting huddled at the window, "Here's Merrie come to see you, dear. Isn't that nice now?"

Aunt Emma had shrunk into a little gray husk, withered and dried up so that I scarcely recognized her. She looked like a sloughed-off skin, discarded when the occupant has moved on.

I ran forward and kissed her and hugged her, but although she smiled and was pleased, there was no spark of recognition in her eyes. A terrible tearing pity shook me, and I sat down beside her and took her hand in mine and stroked it.

Cousin Jessica left us then and went off to dish up the supper, while I sat beside Aunt Emma, her hand held between mine.

"It's been a lovely warm day," she said. "How nice of you to drop in to see me."

I realized that she had no idea who I was.

"I'm Merrie," I said slowly and clearly. "Robert is my father. You remember Robert, don't you?"

"Oh yes, of course I do," said Aunt Emma. "He went away, abroad, you know."

"Yes, and he has come home again and I am his daughter," I explained patiently. "He brought me home with him to live here with you and Cousin Jessica. Don't you remember?"

"I remember his little girl. She was a dear little thing," said Aunt Emma, and her face lit up for a moment. "They called her the little dark thorn, and that wasn't kind of them—but who are *you*, dearie?" she asked.

"I'm *Merrie*," I repeated. "That same little girl who used to live with you, Aunt Emma, only I've grown bigger now."

"Oh no, you can't be that little girl," said Aunt Emma quite sternly, "she died, you know, she was drowned."

"It was *Daisy* who was drowned," I said, "my little sister, Robert and Bergit's child. We all stayed in a cottage in the village last summer and came to see you every day. Surely you remember?"

But she didn't. "Where is Daisy?" she asked. "Isn't she here today?"

I shook my head. I couldn't speak about her any more. Then after a minute, Aunt Emma turned to me again. "And who are you, dearie?" she asked. "I forget so easily."

It was hopeless. Whatever I said, however I tried to explain, she only became more confused. My heart ached for her and I was thankful when Cousin Jessica called up the stairs and we went down to supper.

In bed that night when all the house was still, I lay thinking, first of Aunt Emma and the sad little shadow she had become, then of Daisy and how I had brought her up to this room to play when we came to spend the day in Aunt Emma's house. This room where we had played together only last summer brought her poignantly back to me. I did not want to think about what had happened, and I had to get on with my life. But I did not want to forget Daisy herself, and as long as I could see Bergit's stricken face I could neither forget, nor forgive myself for my part in the tragedy. Yet I hoped that in Aunt Emma's house I would find some peace of mind.

But I had too much time to myself. Too much time to brood. I tried to help Cousin Jessica as much as I could by shopping for her, setting the table and things like that. I could have taken Aunt Emma for walks, but she did not want to go, preferring to sit in the garden with Waterloo beside her. Waterloo, too, was getting old and was not so keen to accompany me on expeditions as once he had been. So I sat in the garden with her part of each day, reading to her, sometimes just talking. Soon I discovered that although she appeared to be listening, she did not take in much of what I was telling her. Like a child listening to a story too old for it, it was the sound of my voice, the attention she enjoyed. Occasionally she knitted in a half-hearted way, but she made lots of mistakes and got annoyed with herself. I would tell her something that I thought would amuse her and for a moment, she would smile and enjoy it, the next, she had forgotten it.

Often she told me about myself when I lived with her, not realizing that *I* was the child she loved.

"Such a small little girl she was," said Aunt Emma. "Prickly and easily upset, but I loved her and I think she loved me in the end."

"I know she did," I replied.

She would ramble on for ages about things that I had done or said, some of them true, some imaginary, but it made her happy to talk about me so I encouraged her to do it.

Sometimes she spoke of my father when he was a boy and lived with her. She made him sound very lovable, and certainly she had loved him dearly.

"It is very strange how sometimes you remind me of Robert, you look like him now," she said.

"It isn't really strange, Aunt Emma, you see I am Robert's daughter, Merrie," I explained once again. But she couldn't accept this, she had it firmly fixed in her mind that Robert's daughter was the small child they'd called the little dark thorn—nothing to do with me.

Soon, I began to confide in Aunt Emma; it was just like talking to myself, it flowed over her, she remembered none of it. I talked to her about Daisy and how desperately I missed her, how I blamed myself for falling asleep when I was in charge of her. I poured out my grief over Bergit, how she had changed, how I feared she would never forgive me. I told her about the mere, and my dread of its dark force, how I had tried to appease it first with Gom and then with the jade water buffalo, peace offerings I had hoped would ward off its evil intent, but I had failed, it had taken Daisy.

"I'm wicked, too," I said. "I did a terrible thing. I allowed my father to think thieves had stolen his jade, when really I had taken it and hidden it in the loft. Now it is at the bottom of the mere. I'll have to tell him about it, and he'll be dreadfully angry. I wish I had told Bergit long ago. Now it's too late, but I must tell *someone*. That's why I'm telling you."

"You're quite right, dearie," said Aunt Emma consolingly, "but who is Bergit?"

This pouring out of my griefs and fears to Aunt Emma did not worry her for she took none of it in, but it did help me a little. It was like going to confession, the telling of it brought me release and a kind of healing, though it did not solve any problems.

18

When I had been at Aunt Emma's for a week and there was no letter from home, I grew more worried about Bergit. Gossie had sent me a post card, but her news was only of the piglets and the farm; she did not mention Bergit's house. I felt really hurt. It looked as if my father, glad to get rid of me, had put me out of his mind. But Bergit, if she had recovered, surely would have written. She knew how terribly unhappy I was. It must mean that she was not better. I could not believe that she, too, had abandoned me.

I longed for someone to turn to, someone wise like Giller, someone who would help me to sort out the mess I was in. Once Aunt Emma could have done it, but not now. There was no one in the village I knew well enough to trust and Cousin Jessica was useless. I thought with longing of Tante Helga and Onkel Lars, if only they weren't so far away, but perhaps now they, too, would never want to see me again.

There seemed to be no one I could depend on, no permanence. Perhaps it was better to trust no one, to count on no one but myself. Deliberately I began to cultivate a hard shell, a rough manner. I adopted a crude way of speaking and even bandied swear words about.

I became the leader of the rougher children, younger than myself, and I plunged into the life of the village up to my ears.

I worked with my school friends at harvest time on the Robinson's farm. Or I borrowed a bicycle and tore about the countryside with Johnny Stone and his school friend Lorrimer, who thought me a savage.

Then I began to see a lot of my old enemy Sammy Green. He was a rough, overgrown boy, loutish and unattractive. I did not care for him at all, but in my hard new mood his very unpleasantness appealed to me. I found it stimulating to quarrel with him; to take up his dares and challenges was exciting. I was much the quicker and cleverer, but he was bigger and stronger than I.

At first we limited ourselves to silly dares, idiotic things like seeing who could hold his breath longest underwater in the deepest pool in the river. Who could walk quickest along the high wall of the doctor's garden. Who could get nearest to the Robinson's bull and tease him with a thorn stick. I was scared of the bull, but I would not let myself be outdone by Sammy Green. We egged one another on to perform more and more dangerous feats, neither of us having the courage or the common sense to refuse the dare.

Gradually our pursuits changed and became more antisocial. I let my hair go wild and my clothing get ragged and dirty. I slopped about with bare feet and sprawled around in as objectionable a way as possible. Aunt Emma didn't seem to notice, but Cousin Jessica was outraged.

"What kind of a scarecrow are you?" she raged. "You're a disgrace! Go and clean yourself, missy, you and that long-haired Sammy Green—you're not fit for decent folks to live with."

Bleat-bleat-bleat. I paid no attention to her. There were worse things she knew nothing about.

Soon we took to nocturnal meetings, activities in the dark were more exciting. After Cousin Jessica had gone to her bed around ten, I crept from my room dressed in jeans and a dark shirt, slipped past Waterloo, and let myself out of the back door, which was never locked anyway. I met Sammy behind the wall of the old forge at the entrance to the village.

At first the excitement of being out at night in the quiet village was enough for us. Now and then car lights warned us to hide. Sometimes we surprised a couple returning from a late stroll, or came upon a pair of lovers so enchanted with one another that they never noticed us. We padded along the village street, dodging from house to house, pausing at a lighted window to peer in, melting into the shadows when someone came out of the inn. The visitors went to the hotel further up the road, only the local people drank at the inn. When it closed, the village went to bed; there was seldom a soul about after eleven o'clock. Sometimes we scouted the wavering light of Bob Rook the policeman coming home late on his bicycle. Sometimes we dived for a ditch as Dr. Stone's car drove along the road on a night call. We would have made good detectives; for, on the nights we were about nothing much happened in the village that we didn't see or hear. We knew how the baker and his wife quarrelled. We stood under their bedroom window listening to their angry voices, and sometimes their blows. From old Bolder's cottage we heard raving and shouting as he acted out in his sleep the nightmares of his war service. We had to be wary and keep out of sight on the nights when Scratt the poacher stole out of his cottage on one of his raids, his eyes and ears were as sharp as any fox and he moved fast and silently.

It was exciting but pretty harmless, although neither Sammy's family nor mine would have approved had they known. We never stayed out for longer than an hour or two; we became too sleepy after that to keep awake. But soon the novelty wore off and we became bored, and that is when trouble began. We began to look around for something more daring, more dangerous, something that would cause a furor if we were caught.

The first thing we did was to open the field gates and let the sheep and cattle out to stray on to the road and up over the hills. Not Mr. Robinson's animals, but those belonging to an ill-tempered farmer further up the valley.

Then we dammed the river and caused a flood in the village street when there was a heavy rainfall overnight.

Another night we pinched all the eggs from the nesting boxes behind the village store and hid them in an unused cottage. Finally, losing our heads completely, we lit a fire in a hay rick and the nearest cottage just escaped the blaze. That brought the policeman in, of course, and we got thoroughly frightened. The morning after this scare, Cousin Jessica was all agog with gossip when she got back from shopping.

"It's not only the rick," she said, "all sorts of queer things have been happening in the village," and she gave me a recital of mischiefs and villainies, most of which had nothing to do with us.

"It must be a tinker," said Cousin Jessica, "one of these wild fellows who live in the hills. Bob Rook is going to keep a lookout for him. He's bringing in a police dog—one of those wolfish Alsatians to patrol the village at night."

"I wonder if they'll catch him?" I remarked. "Has anyone seen him?"

"Not a soul," said Cousin Jessica, "but don't you worry, Mr. Rook may be very slow and not very clever at finding clues, but he won't let us come to any harm."

I smiled inwardly, but I did have the grace to feel ashamed of myself. Sammy had suggested joining a gang down the valley, and I was glad that I had refused. I knew I had been a fool to team up with Sammy Green, whom I didn't like anyway; it had been an act of bravado to prove to myself how tough I had become—but I had found no real satisfaction in what we did.

I warned Sammy about the police dog and that was the end of our nocturnal adventures. I was really glad of the excuse to drop Sammy Green, although I missed the excitement. Bird-watching and fishing were tame substitutes for night-prowling, but I much preferred the company of Johnny Stone and his friend Lorrimer, to that of Sammy Green.

I had my hair cut, washed and patched my tattered jeans, dropped my rough manners and speech, and became myself again.

The summer was coming to an end. I had written to Bergit twice during my time in Aunt Emma's house, but there had been no answer. Soon it would be time to go back to school and I wondered what was to happen to me, so I wrote again saying that I wanted to put things right between us, that I hoped she had forgiven me. My letter was not answered by Bergit but it brought a reply from my father that stunned me. Bergit was ill, really ill. She had gone into a hospital with a breakdown. He had to go abroad on another business trip, so he'd arranged with my headmistress for me to be a boarder. Mrs. Holt would have me at the farm for a few days and would see to my clothes and take me back to school.

His formal letter, so cold and indifferent, froze any kindlier feelings I had had towards him since Daisy's death. As for the news about Bergit's illness, it horrified me. At the same time, it did explain why she had not answered my letters. Perhaps she didn't hate me after all, perhaps the shock and grief of losing Daisy had made her ill and that was why she had seemed so strange and unlike herself.

Poor Bergit, I had been so wrapped up in my own sorrow that I had not understood her. How long had she been in the hospital, I wondered? And why was my father going abroad, leaving her when she was ill and needed him most? I could not understand him; was he utterly heartless after all? And why couldn't he have told me earlier what he was planning for me, instead of settling everything to suit himself and sending me off like a parcel without consulting me?

I had to pack hurriedly and there was not enough time to see all my friends in the village before I left.

When I went to say goodbye to Aunt Emma, I felt very sad to be leaving her. I wondered if the Aunt Emma I had known would have disappeared entirely before I saw her again. When I held out my hands to take hers, she noticed my Malayan bangles, now expanded to their full size, the same ones I had always worn.

"She used to wear bangles," said Aunt Emma smiling. "They tinkled like little bells as she ran about the house. Such a sweet little girl, she was, I wish you had known her, dearie."

I sighed. It was hopeless. "Goodbye, dear Aunt Emma," I said, "and thank you for having me here." I put my arms round her and laid my cheek against hers lovingly.

"Goodbye, dearie, come again soon," she said. "It's strange how much you remind me of Robert."

Dear Aunt Emma—I felt I was saying a last goodbye to her.

19

MRS. HOLT WAS GOOD TO ME, AND GOSSIE WAS STILL AT home, and my own dear Boris was at the farm. So I enjoyed the few days I spent there before I went back to school, although I was worried about Bergit and angry with my father.

Bergit's house was empty, deserted, but Mrs. Holt had the key and she and Gossie went with me to help me to sort out my schoolclothes and pack my trunk. I had no wish to linger there; it was too forlorn, but I did wish I could see Bergit even for a few minutes before I went back to school.

"Where is the hospital Bergit is in?" I asked Mrs. Holt. "Do you think if I went, they'd let me see her?"

"It's Grindlewood Hospital, not far from here; the 18 bus passes the gate," Mrs. Holt told me. "But I'm sure she's not allowed any visitors yet, Merrie—even you. Better wait a bit till your father takes you. You wouldn't want to upset her again, would you?"

"How *ill* is she then?" I asked miserably. "No one's told me a thing about her."

Mrs. Holt put a comforting arm round my shoulder.

"I don't think she's too bad now, lovey," she said. "Your father never really told me much, but I think that when Daisy was drowned, the shock and everything was too much for her, the grief of it finished her—and there were other troubles. Now that she is being taken care of in the hospital, I'm sure she'll soon get better and be able to come home again." Mrs. Holt's kindly words cheered me up a bit, but I wondered what the other troubles were she had hinted at? And when I remembered Bergit's stricken face with all the youth gone out of it, I wondered if she would ever be herself again.

I went back to school in a rebellious state of mind. There was no one there I cared about since Munah left. I was angry with my father for sending me to be a boarder, although under the circumstances I don't know what else he could have done. There was a lot of silly feeling between the day girls and the boarders, who considered themselves the elite. As an ex-day girl I was made to feel an outsider by the boarders until I showed myself worthy of acceptance. What nonsense it all was! It provoked me into making myself felt. I lashed out with a vicious tongue at anyone who approached me. I rebelled against authority and broke every rule, till every teacher found me quite unbearable. I was in trouble all the time, and the more I was reprimanded the worse I became. I upset the girls in my dormitory so much with my bad temper and impossible moods that I was finally given a room to myself.

My father seldom wrote to me, and when he did his letters were formal and official, but he did explain that for some time to come he was likely to be going abroad on business trips, so I must not expect to see him.

Of Bergit I heard nothing, and this was my greatest anxiety for I could not really understand what had happened to her nor why.

It was a remark made by a girl in my class about her own parents that first made me wonder if there might be serious trouble between Bergit and my father. I thought back over the past summer and remembered times before Daisy's death when they had quarrelled over me; there had been tensions and differences, and a change in their close relationship. If there really was a break between them—perhaps this was the other trouble at which Mrs. Holt had hinted—no wonder Bergit, already shattered by Daisy's death, had collapsed. Why had nobody bothered to explain all this to me? There must have been something I could have done to help? Why was I being treated like a child and kept in ignorance?

Somehow I had to see Bergit, provided she was well enough, and find out how much her illness was my fault, how much she blamed me for Daisy's death.

Defiantly I went to my headmistress, Miss Chiswick, and demanded to be allowed to go and see Bergit in the hospital.

Miss Chiswick was reasonable and kind, which I certainly had not expected, and promised to find out if Bergit was allowed visitors yet.

"I think I have a note of the address here—wait a minute —yes: Mrs. Eskin, Room 7, Floor 3, Grindlewood Hospital. I got it from your father before he went abroad. I'll ring the hospital and let you know later. Run along back to work now."

I made a mental note—Room 7, Floor 3—and as I went

back to my classroom I felt a bit more cheerful.

Miss Chiswick sent for me after lessons were over, and I bounded up the stairs to her room full of hope. She asked me to sit down by the fire and took the chair opposite to me. Her manner was a little strange, almost as if she felt embarrassed, and yet sympathetic.

"I'm very sorry to disappoint you, Merrie," she began, "but I'm afraid the hospital can't let you see your mother."

"But why not?" I asked. "Isn't she getting better? She's been there for ages! Surely she's well enough to see me—or doesn't she want to?"

"I think she's a lot better, Merrie, and it isn't that she doesn't want to see you, but . . . well, as a matter of fact, your father left instructions with the hospital that you are not to be allowed to see her till he comes home," said Miss Chiswick.

I gave a little gasp of dismay, and if I hadn't been with Miss Chiswick, I would have stamped my foot angrily.

"I'm sorry, Merrie," Miss Chiswick repeated, "but I'm afraid there's nothing I can do about it. I'm sure your father has a good reason for what he has done. Perhaps he is afraid that a visit from you would distress your mother by reminding her too painfully of what happened; it might slow down her recovery. I'm afraid you'll just have to be patient and wait till your father comes home—it won't be long now. I only wish I could help you."

I thanked her and made my way slowly out of the room. I was boiling inside. I could not understand my father's action, but I was going to ignore it. Miss Chiswick might not be able to do anything about it, but *I* could. I would slip away from school and catch a bus to the hospital and see Bergit! I knew where the hospital was and which bus to catch.

I planned carefully. I would go on a games afternoon

when I would not be easily missed. After having my lunch with the earliest group, I slipped away and out of the gate while the others were changing for games.

I stayed half-hidden in the hedge by the bus stop in case someone from school saw me until the number 18 came along. It was full, but I saw no one on it whom I knew. I bought a ticket to take me as far as the hospital gates and asked the conductor to tell me when we got there.

Half the people on the bus got off at the stop and I walked up the drive with a crowd of other visitors.

"Have you been here before?" a jolly looking woman with a huge bunch of chrysanthemums asked me, and when I told her I hadn't, she asked which floor I wanted.

"Room 7, Floor 3," I told her.

"Same floor as me," she said. "Stay beside me and we can go in together."

I did not tell her that I didn't have permission, of course, and when we joined the group of visitors on Floor 3, waiting for the door to be unlocked, I was glad I had arrived at the right time so that I could slip in unnoticed with the crowd.

As the clock struck two, a starchy looking sister appeared, and a nurse came and unlocked the door in the corridor. I was afraid that they would check the visitors in, and perhaps stop and question me, but like a swarm of gnats, the visitors buzzed through the door and along the corridor, and both the sister and the nurse vanished. I went in with the others and walked on till I saw Room 7, then I tapped on the door and slipped inside.

Bergit was resting, lying asleep fully dressed on the top of her bed; her face was relaxed, and she looked quite well.

"Bergit," I whispered so as not to startle her. "Bergit! It's me."

She opened her eyes and stared at me for a moment and

then her whole face lit up with joy and she held out her arms to me.

"Merrie! Darling Merrie!" she exclaimed hugging me. "I *am* glad to see you. I've been longing for you to come. I haven't been allowed many visitors yet, just one or two friends, but with your father away, you are the one I wanted most. Yet each time I asked Sister to get you here, she made some excuse or other. I'm so glad Miss Chiswick has let you come at last."

"I was waiting to hear that you were well enough for visitors and wanted to see me," I said. Then dropping my voice to a whisper, "Nobody knows I'm here," I added. "I just walked out of school and came!"

Bergit began to giggle. "You're a very naughty girl!" she said lightly. "But oh, I am so happy to see you! Won't you get into trouble for leaving school without permission?"

"I don't care if I do," I said. "It's worth trouble. But I hope I'll be able to slip in again before I am missed. It's a games afternoon you see, and I could be in any of four groups,"

"Merrie! You mustn't do this again," said Bergit laughing. "I'll talk to Sister and when she sees how much good your visit has done me, she'll persuade Miss Chiswick to give you permission to come again, I'm sure."

"I'll come again any time you want me to," I promised, "but it's not Miss Chiswick who won't let me come . . . it's . . . father!"

Bergit looked astonished, and her face hardened.

"What on earth—" she began, then seemed to change her mind. "Perhaps he thought you'd upset me or something," she said. "But now that I'm so much better, nearly well again in fact, nobody need stop you coming. I'll arrange it."

"When will father be home?" I asked. "And when are you coming out of the hospital? Shall we all be together for Christmas?"

Bergit laughed. "What a lot of questions," she said. "And I have the same answer to all of them—I don't know. Now tell me how you are getting on at school. What's it like being a boarder?"

I didn't tell her anything really, except what would make her laugh. I did not want her to know how miserable I felt, so I kept off serious subjects.

"I'd better not stay much longer," I said finally. "I must get back to school before I'm missed, and I don't want to tire you. I haven't done you any harm by coming, have I?" I asked anxiously.

"No, you've cheered me up a lot, but you mustn't ever again visit a patient in a hospital without permission," she said gravely. "And I advise you to go and confess to Miss Chiswick when you get back to school."

"You will arrange for me to come again? Mrs. Holt would bring me on a weekend I'm sure—that's to say if you really want to see me?" I said.

"Of course I want to see you, silly," said Bergit gently. "You do get some queer ideas into your head! You're my daughter, aren't you, my *only* daughter now, and very precious. Why wouldn't I want to see you?" I hugged her joyfully, it was just what I wanted to hear.

"Then you'll arrange it, won't you?" I urged. "As soon as you can. Darling Bergit, I must go! See you soon."

I slipped out and along the corridor without meeting a soul. The nurses all seemed to be getting tea ready, judging by the clatter of cups in the kitchen.

I was lucky with a bus and by teatime I was standing in the queue at school with the others, waiting for the tea bell.

As Bergit advised, I went to see Miss Chiswick that evening and confessed what I had done. She didn't seem particularly surprised nor annoyed, and I did not get the lecture I had expected—perhaps Sister had forestalled me.

"Come and tell me first before you carry out your next idea," she said crisply. "I might be able to help you. Will a cup of coffee keep you awake? There's more than an hour till bedtime, and I'd like to hear about your mother. How is she?"

Before I knew what I was doing, I was sitting by Miss Chiswick's fire, sipping a cup of very good coffee and talking to her quite freely. I found myself telling her things I had meant to keep bottled up inside me, and it was surprising how much she seemed to understand about my difficulties without being told.

"Fathers don't like to see their daughters growing up. It's quite usual, and we have to make allowances for them," she assured me when I complained about my father treating me like a child. "Of course, a daughter has to learn to conduct herself in a grown-up manner so that eventually her father will accept the fact that she is no longer a child. Living with us here, away from home and on your own, is giving you the chance to grow up. Perhaps it will be good for your father and your mother, when she is better, to have a little time to themselves. The past summer has been very sad and deeply disturbing to you all. Don't you think your parents may need to be alone together for a while to settle down again?"

However dry and matter of fact Miss Chiswick's manner might be, what she said made good sense, and she was surprisingly understanding. When I said goodnight and left her room, I felt that a turning point had been reached. I was more hopeful and more assured about the future.

What Miss Chiswick had said about my father stuck in

my mind, and I found myself thinking of him in a different way that was less critical and more detached. I felt ready to make allowances and to meet him halfway when he came home.

20

MRS. HOLT WAS A GOOD FRIEND TO US, AND DURING THOSE
weeks before my father came home I spent every Saturday
or Sunday at the farm and she took me over to the hospital
and left me with Bergit. When it was fine, we walked in the
grounds and gardens; when it was wet, we sat in Bergit's
room. Then her hospital treatment was finished and she
was ready to leave. My father was not yet home, so once
again Mrs. Holt came to our rescue and took Bergit back to
the farm with her. From there she went home for a few
hours each day, and with Mrs. Peters' help, got the house
cleaned and ready for occupation. It was a breaking-in pe-
riod while she got used to living a normal life again after her
months in the hospital.

On the weekends I was able to help her, too, to turn our
house into a home again.

We were almost on our old terms of affection and closeness, happy to be together. We spoke Norwegian when we were alone. I did not want to forget it, and many a good laugh we had over the mistakes I made. But I did not yet dare to speak of the sad times behind us, of Daisy's death, of Bergit's illness, and of the upsets with my father. These were subjects best left alone, the wounds were too newly healed to touch.

Once Bergit was out of the hospital, I noticed a difference in her. She had always been reserved, but now she seemed timid. There was a new nervousness about her. Where once there had been strength and purpose, there was wavering indecision, a lack of self-confidence. Gradually I realized that although she *looked* all right, she had been through a terrible time and it might take months before she was completely well again. Loving her as I did, I felt staunchly protective towards her. I did not risk upsetting her by asking difficult questions, it was enough for the moment that we were happy together.

I wondered how much my father would understand this unfamiliar Bergit, whether he would be kind and patient enough to help her to recover. I worried about whether they'd be able to put their marriage right again, but I kept my anxieties to myself.

There were only two weeks of the term left when my father came home to Bergit's house and I began to count the days till Christmas. I pictured the three of us at home together, leading ordinary lives again, free from drama, uncomplicated by our old troubles. It was a picture seen through a rosy glass, and I knew that it was largely make-believe.

Even now I don't know what went so hopelessly wrong, but the end soon came to my cozy domestic dream. Two days before the term finished, I had a letter from Bergit. It was very short and quite final. She told me that she was going home to Norway at once and was very distressed not to see me before she left. Mrs. Holt would have me for the Christmas holidays, and my father was leaving for Australia on business immediately.

"I'm terribly sorry, darling," she wrote, "but I'm not very well and there's nothing else I can do at the moment. But don't worry, I *promise* I will bring you out to Norway as soon as I can."

It was a bitter blow, unexpected and hard. Everything seemed to have fallen apart just when I had begun to hope that the worst was over.

It must have been a very sudden and quick decision, for Miss Chiswick sent for me later in the day to tell me she had had a rushed call from my father after Bergit had already gone and as his plane was about to leave. I felt bitterly disappointed that he hadn't even made time to speak to me on the phone, and although Miss Chiswick gave me various nice messages from him, I half-suspected she had made them up.

"Will he be away for long this time?" I asked. "His business seems to have become terribly important to him." Much more important than Bergit or me I thought to myself.

"He said he thought your mother had come out of the hospital too soon. He thinks she needs a long convalescence to get perfectly well again, and this seemed a good chance for him to accept the excellent offer his firm had made him of a trip to Australia and the Far East. He knows you'll be happy at the farm with Mrs. Holt for the holidays. He said he'll write to you and send your Christmas present later. Don't take it too hard, my dear. I know it's a big disappointment, but you are old enough to be sensible and to appreciate the difficulties."

Wise Miss Chiswick, she had said the right thing to build up my precarious self-esteem.

There was so much to do those last two days with the school party, the carol singing in the frosty darkness, the packing up and the final goodbyes that I had no time to fret. On a wave of pre-Christmas excitement I left in the car with Gossie and Mrs. Holt.

Snow fell on Christmas Eve, heavy continuous snow, drifting steadily down, piling up along the window and door ledges, padding the roofs, filling up the lane to the road so that Mr. Holt had to get his tractor out and clear it away before we could get the car along it to go to church on Christmas morning.

Friends and neighbors kept coming in and out of the big farm kitchen all day. Although Mrs. Holt tried to lure them into the "parlor," as she called it, in the front of the house, it was in the warm kitchen with its big stove, its cheerful glinting copper and its wonderful smells of cooking that everyone seemed to congregate.

Christmas dinner for fifteen at six o'clock was the highlight of the day, and after that we all gathered round the Christmas tree to sing carols by candlelight.

Later, one of the young farmers got out his accordion and began to play, and in no time we were all dancing. Even the older people joined in until they got too tired and retired to gossip round the fire or to watch television in the front room.

When eventually bedtime came, and the last of the guests had gone out into the snow, Gossie and I, our arms round one another's waists, climbed the stairs to her room. What a happy day it had been, and what good friends the Holts were to me! We were almost too sleepy to get undressed, and Gossie was into bed first and asleep before I could even say goodnight to her. By that time I was too contented and drowsy myself to feel more than a passing regret for the Christmas we might have had at home in Bergit's house, and I had only a brief thought to spare for my father baking in the Australian summer. Though once I was in bed, memories of Bergit filled my mind—how I missed her! I pictured her in the farm house above the fjord, in the Norwegian kitchen I knew so well with its softly gleaming wood, its candlelit table, its scent of the pine forests, and its people whom I loved. Surely there, with Tante Helga and Onkel Lars, in the heart of her family and friends, Bergit would find again her security and her happiness—this was my Christmas wish to her.

I got to know Gossie very well during those Christmas holidays. Sharing a room with her meant that we were able to talk more intimately than ever before. She had slimmed down into an attractive girl, handsome rather than pretty, and since she was older than I, she would be leaving school in the summer.

"What will you do then, Gossie?" I asked. "Go to agricultural college?"

"No need for that, father says," Gossie replied. "There's plenty to do on the farm here, and later on I'll marry some young farmer chap—one of our neighbors likely. A farmer's wife is what I'll be."

She had it all planned out; she would make a good and comfortable wife for some "young farmer chap," a life practical and contented. Her future seemed to run ahead along a familiar, well-marked path, while mine like a dust track, wandered off into the wilderness.

The snow lasted the whole of the holidays and every day we joined a group of boys and girls from the village and the neighboring farms on one of the long hills which sloped from the downs to the valley. There we tobogganed or made slides, shouting with laughter and snowballing one

another. Sometimes we played on the village pond, skating
or sliding on the ice, which had been tested and declared
safe by some of the older men.

Although the mere was frozen over, its black heart im-
prisoned under the ice, no one ever skated there. It was a
bad place, its reputation evil, it was always considered
treacherous and dangerous; everyone avoided it.

When the day's fun was over and the red sun dipped behind the bare black trees, the first stars sharp with frost
drove us indoors; a dozen of us or more would crowd into
the farm kitchen, ravenous for one of Mrs. Holt's splendid
teas. Later there was television or letters to write to Bergit
or Aunt Emma, or sometimes we went out to a party. Often
friends came in for the evening for a game of cards, and
Gossie and I made the coffee and helped to pass the homemade cider. Life seemed to run sweetly and evenly in the
Holts' home, there was no apparent tension or strain, although like everyone else, they must have had their bad
times. By drawing me into their family life and making me
feel so much one of them, I had been made to feel I belonged.

Suddenly it all came to an end, Gossie and I packed up
and went back to our schools. I wished we could have
stayed together.

Only once before I left the farm, did I make my way to
Bergit's house to have a look at it. Although I knew that
Mrs. Peters went in regularly to keep it clean and aired, the
house had a deserted forlorn look. It seemed as if the heart
had gone out of it. But more than that, I had the impres-
sion that it felt itself discarded.

My holiday at Holt's Farm had been such a happy one
that I went back to school in a very different mood. To begin with, I admired and liked Miss Chiswick, and knew I
could count on her help and interest. I was becoming more

sure of myself, too, and I was ready to make friends with the other girls. Those in the new dormitory I was put into were likeable and uncritical. Most of the staff made it clear that last term's troubles were forgotten and they were ready for me to make a fresh beginning. In fact, I had turned over a new leaf and the atmosphere was one of expectancy and promise.

Shortly after term began, I had a lovely surprise.

There was a parcel from Hong Kong addressed in my father's writing. I tore it open and shook out a beautiful dress. It was made of silk and embroidered all over with flowers. When I tried it on, it fit me perfectly and the other girls were full of envy.

"It's gorgeous!" one of them cried. "You must wear it at the next party."

There was a card with it from my father apologizing that it was late for Christmas and hoping I'd like it and wear it.

I was simply delighted with my present and touched that my father should have taken the trouble to find something so lovely. He must certainly have been thinking of me then, so perhaps I *did* matter to him after all.

I sat down and wrote to him at once to thank him and to tell him how thrilled I was, but I had to go to Miss Chiswick for his firm's address so that my letter would be sent on to him. I thought over what I had said in my letter for a long time before I posted it. I hoped I had expressed myself as I wanted to. I wondered if he would understand that I wanted to make a fresh start with him. "Please come and see me as soon as you get home," I wrote. I wanted to show him that I was ready to be friends with him, to meet him halfway.

To Bergit I wrote regularly, telling her the little ups and downs of my days and sending messages to Tante Helga and Onkel Lars and to my other friends in Norway. I did not have many letters back. I think Bergit found it an effort to write, and although she said she was getting better every day, she did not sound really happy.

It was the middle of February before my father came to see me. It was a very wet Saturday, the snow had gone but it had left the whole earth sodden.

I dressed carefully in the best clothes I had at school and tried to make myself look as attractive as possible. My heart was beating fast as I waited for him at the window of the entrance hall.

He arrived in a new car, and I ran to open the front door as he hurried up the steps through the pouring rain.

"Merrie!" he cried, kissing my cheek. "Let me look at you. Good heavens, child, you look much older . . . almost grown-up!" I knew that he was half-teasing me, but I was pleased.

"Well, it's seven months since you saw me, so of course I look older," I replied laughing. "I'm nearly sixteen, you know."

He looked well himself, but his hands were icy, and I pulled him over to the fire to get warm. I knew that he was nervous. I was glad to see him, but we were shy of one another, and I wondered what we would find to say.

"What a pity it's such a ghastly day," he said brightly. "Shall we go now, or do I have to see Miss Chiswick first?"

"She said after we get back," I said. "I suppose I must put my mac on. Where are we going?"

"I've booked a table for lunch at The Crown and I thought perhaps a film afterwards? D'you like the car? It's an office one. I've borrowed it for the day."

"Smashing!" I cried heartily. "Let's go."

It was certainly a marvellous car, smooth and expensive looking. The office must be doing very well, I thought.

It was a super lunch, quite wonderful after school food,

and I did my best to be entertaining and to cover up my shyness. About his travels he was enthusiastic and interesting, and so long as we stuck to what might be called "outside" topics we got on pretty well. But towards the end of lunch, I tried to broach "inside" matters. There were so many questions I was longing to ask him, but I did not want to spoil his friendly mood.

"How is Aunt Emma?" I began. "She never answers my letters, but I expect she forgets to."

"She's getting worse, I'm afraid," he said. "Dr. Stone says Cousin Jessica can't look after her any more, so I'm going up there next week to move her into a home with other old people, and Cousin Jessica is going to live with a sister in Northumberland."

"Oh dear, how sad, poor Aunt Emma. I wonder if she'll mind? Actually, she probably won't remember where she is," I remarked, "so she may be quite happy if she has her own things around her in her room. What will happen to the house? I suppose it will be sold?"

My father nodded. "As soon as possible," he said.

"I hate to think of other people living in Aunt Emma's house!" I exclaimed. "Don't you? It was your home for far longer than it was mine."

"What can I do with it but sell it?" he asked. "I can't afford to keep it as a holiday house, much as I'd like to. It's got to be sold. Come along now, or we'll miss the beginning of the film." Obviously he was determined to avoid any more intimate talk about the things that mattered to us both.

The film took up all the afternoon; it was not good enough to keep me absorbed, and I kept worrying about how I was going to find out the things I had to know.

Over tea it would have to be, perhaps by then he would be more approachable.

The tea shop we went to was busy, and we had to share a table, but I plucked up my courage and asked, "Where are you staying just now? At home?"

"No, I'm in a hotel in London till I go abroad again," he said shortly.

"And when will that be?"

"Any time now, after I've been up to Cumberland. I'm likely to be away again for nearly six months," he said.

"So you won't be here for the Easter holidays?" I asked.

"No. I thought you'd like to go to the Holts, as a paying guest, of course. You like being there, don't you?"

"Very much," I agreed. "But I'd hoped . . . Bergit might be home by then."

I had a sudden piercing longing to be at home, to be sitting at the kitchen table munching hot buttered toast, all three of us.

"No, Bergit won't be back . . . not for some time," said my father shortly.

"But she's getting better isn't she?" I broke in anxiously. "She'll soon be well enough to come home, surely?"

"It may be a long time till she is . . . ready to come home again," said my father. "It is better for her to be with her parents just now." Abruptly he began to speak of something else.

It was no explanation. He was treating me like a small child, but I could see he was not going to tell me anything more. I did not want to spoil the day by quarreling with him, so I controlled my tongue and did not probe any further. I remembered what Miss Chiswick had said about fathers. After all, he was doing his best to give me a happy time, and I felt grateful to him for trying. I hoped that next time he came there would be less stiffness, less awkwardness between us and we'd be able to get closer to one another.

"It was a lovely dress you sent me from Hong Kong," I

said, returning to safer ground. "I often take it out and look at it although I have not worn it yet."

"I'm very glad," he said. "I thought it would make a pretty party dress for you. I'm going to India next; I'll have to find something for you there, a piece of ivory perhaps?"

"Oh thank you, I'd love that," I said, and a fearful feeling of guilt stabbed me as I was reminded of the little jade water buffalo and how I had deceived him about it; but this was not the moment to confess.

"I suppose we'd better get you back to school. I've got to see your headmistress in her den," he said ruefully. "I hope she won't devour me!"

I laughed loudly as I assured him that Miss Chiswick was no dragon.

"What about a box of chocolates to take back with you?" he suggested. He bought me the biggest one he could find and gave me some extra pocket money. It hurt me to see him trying so hard to please me, to make up to me for the things I was missing, when all I wanted was to break down the barrier between us so that we could be friends. In spite of his abrupt and rather distant manner, I knew that he was concerned about me, for as we drove back to school, he questioned me in a kindly way. "You *are* all right, aren't you—at school, I mean, and with the Holts?"

"Oh yes, I'm all right," I assured him. "I like Miss Chiswick very much and the Holts of course, but . . . oh it would be wonderful to be at home again with Bergit and you!" It came out with a rush and I was afraid I had said too much. He didn't answer me and turned his head away; perhaps that's what he wanted, too, only he would never allow himself to say so.

In an uneasy silence we drove through the gates and along the drive to the door. He hurried me up the steps, and I took him straight to Miss Chiswick's room.

"I'll wait for you in the hall," I said.

I went and stood beside the fire to warm myself. I was trembling with a sense of failure, of disappointment, and yet I dreaded saying goodbye to him.

Miss Chiswick kept him for some time, but at last I heard her door open and they came down the stairs, chatting together in a friendly way. She brought him over to me, shook hands with him and put her arm round my shoulders for a moment, then left us.

I don't know what she had said to him, but somehow she had broken through his guard. His expression had softened and relaxed; he looked . . . vulnerable, defenseless. I remembered the time I had found him in the barn after Daisy died, and the same feeling I had for him then swept through me now. Impulsively, I threw my arms round his neck and clung to him, choking back my tears.

"It's been a *lovely* day," I gulped. "Thank you for being so good to me. I wish you weren't going away. I wish . . . oh please let's all be at home together in Bergit's house again soon, *please*."

"We'll try, Merrie," he said gently. "We'll try, I promise." He kissed my cheek and held me lovingly for a moment before he left me and went out into the rain.

I stood at the window watching him out of sight, comforted by the closeness of his last few minutes. I wished I had been able to break through his reserve sooner—his and mine, so that we could have talked. Perhaps I could have made him understand how much I cared about what happened between Bergit and him. Well, I had tried and failed; he had refused to give anything away, even to talk about Bergit's illness. Daisy's death had never been mentioned since the day it happened.

"What will happen to us next?" I wondered as I went sadly upstairs.

21

My father's visit was not what I had hoped for, but I really had enjoyed being with him. We had tried to please one another; we had managed to avoid quarreling, and at the end there had been the few moments of closeness, of warmth, and of truth between us. Certainly a step forward had been made in our relationship. And I had learned something about myself: in spite of all our difficulties and irritations with one another, deep down I could really care about him. Perhaps next time we met it would be easier, if only we didn't have too long to wait before we saw each other again.

At least he rang me to say goodbye before he left. He told me that Aunt Emma seemed quite happy in the home for old people he had taken her to. His voice on the phone was crisp and businesslike, as if he was too rushed for a gentler mood he had shown me earlier.

Six months he expected to be away—six months was a long time, anything could happen. Our future looked uncertain; with Bergit in Norway, myself at boarding school, my father traveling round the earth, and our home shut up. How were we ever going to come together again? Miss Chiswick rescued me from my depression with a piece of good advice.

"Get your teeth into something that will absorb you and take up your attention, music perhaps, or a craft, ceramics? Even one of your regular school subjects like history," she said.

Luckily for me, I respected her judgment and did what she suggested. I began to work, really work, at my ordinary school subjects for the first time in my life. To my enormous surprise, I enjoyed it, and little by little I became absorbed in history and then in English. Unexpected windows opened for me, and I found I was fascinated even by some of the subjects I had considered dull. Of course, there were certain classes, like math, which I loathed and they simply had to be got through. Math, I could never enjoy.

There must have been a very marked improvement in my work, for before the end of term, Miss Chiswick moved me up a class and praised my efforts.

"If you go on like this and do some work in the Easter holidays and perhaps have coaching in math," she said, "I see no reason why you shouldn't have a shot at some 'O' levels in the summer. I've always known you were intelligent. Now let's see what you can do. I'll write to your father at once. I know he'll be pleased."

I had heard from him twice from India, interesting but drily impersonal letters, and mine back had been carefully detached, but at least they kept a cobweb thread of contact between us, which was better than nothing. But after he got

Miss Chiswick's letter, and mine telling him I had been moved up a class and would be working for exams, he wrote to me quite differently. He seemed really delighted and urged me to have extra coaching in the holidays, which Miss Chiswick would arrange for me. His approval meant more to me than I had reckoned on, and I determined to do my best.

The Easter holidays at the farm streaked past as I worked at the books set for my exams and had the necessary coaching. This took up a lot of my time, and Gossie would have found me a poor companion if she had not been so taken up with her first boy friend, a young man who lived in the village.

As often as possible, I took Boris for walks on the downs, and alone with him I had a chance to think about my future and to try to decide what I wanted to do.

Before I went back to school, I wrote a long letter to Bergit begging her to let me spend the summer holidays with her in Norway.

Her answer came back by return mail, telling me that she and her parents would love to have me and that she was writing to my father about it.

Then and there I sat down and wrote to him myself asking him to let me go.

I was hard at work in school again before his reply came, but when it did, it was, "Yes!" I was thrilled. It would be wonderful to go back to Norway and to spend the holidays there with Bergit. I worked with every ounce of energy I possessed, and when the time of the "O" level exams came, I felt I hadn't done too badly.

Term crawled to its end as I crossed off the days on my calendar, and at last it was all over and I went to the farm for a few nights. Mrs. Holt, who had a key, went along with me to Bergit's house. I wanted to collect some summer clothes to take away with me, if any of them still fit.

"How long will you be?" asked Mrs. Holt. "I must get back soon to my jam-making."

"Not more than half an hour," I said, "but please don't go."

"Well, I'll open a few windows and dust round a little while I'm waiting," said Mrs. Holt. The house smelled fusty and airless, as old houses do when they are shut up. It didn't feel like home any more.

I picked out an extra sweater, shorts, a couple of shirts, a cotton frock or two, and stuffed them into a bag. They were all rather worn and a bit juvenile for me, but I meant to go shopping the next day and spend some of the money my father had sent me for the holidays.

Before I left the room I took a last look round and laid a caressing hand on Daisy's bed. Then I hurried up to the attic, to my corner by the window and lifted up the board, the hiding place of my treasures. They were all there, except Gom and the little jade—all safely hidden. I put the board back and stood looking out of the window. The haze of midsummer gave the scene an ethereal beauty, a quality of unreality like an old print, faded and past.

Even the mere looked tranquil and ordinary. It no longer had the power to frighten me. I felt detached, uninvolved, as if I had come to the end of a path and found a new road stretching ahead of me, enticing and untried.

"I wonder . . . if we'll ever . . . live . . . in Bergit's house . . . again?" I said aloud.

"Are you ready, Merrie?" called Mrs. Holt as I ran downstairs.

"Yes," I cried, "shall we go?"

She shut the windows and I locked the door and put the

key in my pocket.

"It's such a pity, the house and everything," she murmured shaking her head. "I try to go in once in a while just to keep an eye on things, but . . . well . . . there's nothing much *anyone* can do. And all that fruit going to waste in the orchard! It's a shame I can't use more of it. But I'm ever so glad you're going to Bergit, lovey; it'll do you both good to be together."

As we walked back to the farm along the path by the boat house, I noticed several piles of half-dried weeds rotting on the bank of the mere. How on earth had they gotten there? Negligently I kicked one with my foot as I passed, scattering the heap . . . and my toe met something hard. A stone? Perhaps a broken bottle? My curiosity was aroused. I dropped my bag on the path, fell on my knees and began scrabbling among the slime of the rotted weed. My fingers cautiously prodded till I found it, hard, cold, smooth. It was not a stone, nor a bottle . . . it was the little jade water buffalo!

I gave a cry of amazed delight, and I wiped the mud off it and dipped it into the water to clean it properly.

"Look!" I cried to Mrs. Holt as I dried it with my handkerchief, "just look what I've found! How on earth did it get here? I threw it into the mere as far out as I could. I never dreamed I'd see it again, ever."

"You *threw* it into the mere?" repeated Mrs. Holt incredulously. "What on earth made you do that?"

"I did it in a moment of panic and fear," I said. "What I can't understand is how it came to be on the bank in a pile of weed?"

"There have been campers in the field on the other side," said Mrs. Holt. "They had a rubber dinghy, so maybe they went fishing with a net or a pole."

"Perhaps that was it, a sort of dragnet, and they emptied out the weed without examining it!" I exclaimed.

I held the little jade on the palm of my hand, turning it about, observing it closely, critically—it was quite unharmed. I couldn't believe it was there in my grasp. It was a kind of miracle! A magic.

"It's a beautiful little thing, isn't it?" said Mrs. Holt admiringly. "You're very lucky indeed to have it back. Are you coming now? I've got to get on with my jam, and the men will be in for their tea."

"You go on," I said. "I'll follow you soon, but there's something I've got to do first."

"All right, lovey, don't be too long, and be sure to lock up properly if you go back to the house," said Mrs. Holt. "I'll take your bag for you." She picked it up and went on towards the farm.

I rose to my feet, holding the little jade against my cheek. I couldn't believe it was true, the mere had given it back to me! Gratefully I turned to face the water and bowed ceremoniously. "Thank you," I said aloud. "Thank you very much indeed."

Suddenly I felt light-hearted, gay, unburdened, and I knew what I must do.

I ran up the path to Bergit's house, unlocked the door and went quickly up to the attic. I kissed the little jade, then I hid it in my old hole under the floor boards with my other treasures. I had made an important decision. I had decided to give it back to my father next time he was at home and to tell him the whole story. Perhaps if we could talk about it, we would come to a better understanding.

I felt better then. It was much more than giving back something that did not belong to me, something that had meant so much to me. It was turning away from bitterness, turning towards forgiveness, it was relinquishing a child-hood fantasy and facing up to reality. It was my promise to the future.

I walked out of the house, locked the front door, and found Boris waiting for me in the garden. Together we raced along the path by the mere, back to the farm for tea.

Next day, Mrs. Holt and Gossie took me to the airport to see me off. I was wearing my new clothes and hoped I looked at least seventeen.

While I waited for my flight to Bergen, Gossie and I were poking around the bookstall, when suddenly a voice behind me exclaimed, "Merrie! What a nice surprise!" It was Miss Chiswick leaving for a holiday in Yugoslavia, and I intro-duced Gossie to her.

"I didn't recognize you at first, you look so grown-up. I wish your father could see you as you are now—poor man, he'd get a shock!" she said laughing. "I must be off, have a happy holiday, my dear, and give my best wishes to your mother. Goodbye till September."

At that moment my flight number went up on the board, and I had to leave Gossie and Mrs. Holt and hurry to the departure lounge, then into the plane.

As we roared off the ground and climbed high into the air, I looked down on the miniature fields and villages of England. I had the curious sensation of having left part of myself behind, something no longer vital that I had dis-carded, like a sloughed-off skin that had become too tight for me. "Perhaps it is all part of growing up," I thought.

Part III
Merrie's House

22

Bergit was at the airport to meet me looking wonderfully well, golden and young, but she was thinner and her expression was a little sad. When she spotted me, her face lit up, and we ran to one another with outstretched arms.

"Bergit! Oh Bergit! You don't know how much I've been looking forward to this!"

"Merrie, my darling, is it really you? Let me look at you —how you've grown up, and how pretty you are! It's wonderful to have you here."

We got through the customs quickly and piled my luggage into the waiting car.

Soon we were out of the town and driving inland, and I found myself chattering to Bergit in Norwegian.

It was lovely to be back in Norway. The country was all just as I remembered it—the pretty white or gray houses round the little churches, like toy villages, the long lines of hay drying in the sun, the small cream-colored horses. And as we climbed higher, mountains and fjords spread out before us and I remembered the tiny bridges swinging over the streams of rushing mountain water, the forests of dark fir trees, and the neat stacks of wood piled along the road sides.

After a while we stopped talking. There was plenty of time for that later on, and Bergit had to concentrate on driving, for the roads became still narrower and more twisting. I was happy just to be with her and to enjoy this country that I had learned to love.

It was evening by the time we saw the mountain behind Bergit's home. Bergit slowed the car to a gentler pace as we drove along the cliff road above the fjord.

"There it is! There's the farm," I cried excitedly as we emerged from one of the tunnels cut through the rock, "and there's Tante Helga and Onkel Lars sitting outside the door."

They gave me a wonderful welcome and led me into the old wooden farmhouse with its slated roof and silver-gray walls. I climbed the polished staircase, past the painted grandmother chest, to the little room under the eaves where I had slept on my first visit to Norway.

Bergit came up and sat on my bed while I unpacked, asking me about the Holts and Mrs. Peters, about school and our shopkeepers in the village, about Boris and the farm, about our house and friends—a hundred things she wanted to know, little details that showed me how much she was missing her life in England. But she did not speak of my father.

When I was ready, we went down together to the big kitchen. The candles of welcome were alight on the table, and there was fish from the fjord for supper. Tante Helga's sister Sophie was staying with them; she was a lively old woman and very like Tante Helga.

While we were eating, we talked about the people I remembered, the men who worked for Onkel Lars on the farm, some of the neighboring farmers, and friends in the village. We spoke in Norwegian and Onkel Lars was very pleased that I had not forgotten it.

"And the little house with the grass roof where I used to play, is it still there?" I asked.

"Certainly it is," Tante Helga assured me, and there was a twinkle in her eye.

"How are the Petersens?" I asked, "Anders and Mr. Petersen? Erik and Inga?"

"Merrie, didn't you know?" said Tante Helga, suddenly grave. "Inga is dead. I thought Bergit had told you. It is more than two years now since Nils Petersen died; we miss him very much, but Inga's sudden death in the fall was a dreadful shock to all of us, a tragedy. She caught a cold, which went into pneumonia, and not even the modern drugs could save her. She has left Erik with two young children to bring up and only old Margit to help him. Bergit has been going over there a lot to help with the children. It is very hard for them."

"I'm terribly sorry," I said. "What a dreadful thing to happen. I remember Inga and Erik very well, although they were not married when I was here."

Erik Petersen, such a handsome young giant of a man, and Inga so gay and pretty. How happy they had been together, both students when last I saw them, engaged to be married and planning their future. Now Inga was gone and Erik left alone—it was a cruel ending to a happy marriage. I wondered about the children, I knew how much they must miss their mother. I was glad that Bergit had been looking after them.

When supper was over and I had helped Bergit to clear away, Tante Helga would not let me do any more. "Take the child up to bed, Bergit," she said. "She must be very tired." I was glad to say goodnight; I felt quite exhausted after all the excitement of the day. Bergit stayed with me while I undressed, and when I got into bed, she tucked me in and kissed me goodnight, just as she had done when I was a little girl, and it made me feel very happy.

Bergit took me across the fields next day to the Petersen farm to see Erik and his children. He was as handsome as ever but rather silent and grave, and he looked much older than I remembered him. The children were sweet. Nils, called after his grandfather, was four, and Kari the little girl was only three. The old woman, Margit, who looked after them did her best, but I saw from the way the children clung to Bergit and their delight at being with her, how much they missed their young mother. I wanted to make up to these children for what they had lost. When Bergit went to the Petersens again I accompanied her, I wanted to be with the children and to help in any way I could.

The first week of my holiday slipped by and was gone almost before I noticed it; there was so much to do, such nice people to see. I helped with the haymaking, and played with the goats when Tante Helga went to milk them, and I rode in the fields on the pale ponies.

It was a late summer, and everyone made the most of enjoying the sun. We were out all day long.

I went to look at the little house with the grass roof where I had played, and found that it had been repaired. The door was locked and a curtain was drawn across the window so that I could not even peep in. It looked very neat indeed.

"Someone must be living in it," I said to myself. "Perhaps someone who works on the farm."

Sometimes when she was not busy, Bergit and I climbed up through the woods behind the farm and took our lunch with us. We spread ourselves out in the sun and lay talking or drowsing peacefully. Little by little we uncovered the griefs and silences of the past year. It was an enormous relief to be able to talk to her freely again.

"When Daisy was drowned, I thought it was my fault," I confessed. "I thought you and father blamed me for not watching her more carefully. I thought you'd never forgive me or want to see me again and that's why you sent me away—it was awful!"

"Oh my poor Merrie, it was *myself* I blamed, not you! I was overwhelmed at what had happened, as any mother would have been. I was so shut up in my own unhappiness that I never gave a thought to what you might be going through. You must forgive me."

"So it wasn't all my fault, the accident and your illness and . . . everything?" I faltered.

"Of course not," cried Bergit. "Nobody blamed you, it was no one's fault. It is all behind us now, and we've got to make a fresh start."

I gave a deep sigh of relief.

As we went on talking I told her about my terror of the mere, of my sense of disaster and how I had tried to avert it.

"I stole the little jade water buffalo. I let you and my father think the burglars had taken it, but it was me. I threw it into the mere as a kind of peace offering. But it didn't work and now the mere has given it back to me," I said. I explained how I had found it on the bank.

"I've hidden it in my place in the attic for safety till I can give it back to my father," I told her.

As she listened to my story, slow tears slid down Bergit's cheeks. "Darling Merrie, how you *torment* yourself," she murmured.

"Not any more," I said. "I've left it all behind me. Something new has begun. I think I'm growing up at last."

"I *know* you are," said Bergit. "You're bursting out of your old ideas as you are out of that old frock!"

There was only one subject we never discussed. Although we spoke quite often about my father, the break in their marriage was never mentioned. It was obvious that Bergit did not want to talk about it, even to me. I could not ask her why it had happened, nor how much I was to blame for it, nor could I question her about the future. I had to be content to wait, to hope that they'd be able to find happiness together again.

Then one morning there was a letter for Bergit from my father in England—he was home again. There were messages in it for me, which Bergit read out to me along with the general news. It was a long letter, and after breakfast Bergit went up to her room by herself, while I went to milk the goats for Tante Helga.

I had just finished when I saw Bergit hurrying up the hill to meet me.

"I'm going back," she cried, "back to England, back to your father, Merrie!" It was as if his letter had given her the impetus she needed to make up her mind and had somehow set her free.

"Oh, I'm so *glad!*" I cried hugging her joyfully. "It's just what I've been longing for. When will you go?"

"At once, tomorrow. I've sent him a telegram. You'll be all right here with my parents for the rest of the holidays, won't you?" she asked.

"Of course," I replied at once. "You know I love it here,

and you and father must have some time to be alone together," I added quoting Miss Chiswick. "But it *will* be all
right, won't it. You can put everything right between you?"

"Yes, it'll be all right," said Bergit. "It's *got* to be."

Later I made her promise to bring Boris from the farm,
and I sent messages to Mrs. Holt and Gossie. "Tell her I'll
write," I said, "and tell father, too, and . . . give him my
love."

She was gone next morning and although I missed her, I
had a great feeling of gladness. At last things were beginning to go right for us all.

I took my sewing out on to the porch and sat down beside Tante Helga and her sister.

"Well, Bergit's gone at last," said Tante Helga. "She
waited for a long time."

"Sometimes I've wondered if she'd ever go back to Robert," Tante Sophie remarked.

"You don't mind being left with us do you, Merrie? We
love having you here," said Tante Helga. "Bergit and your
father need to be alone together for a while. . . . There
have been . . . complications."

"Yes, I know. I'm one of the complications," I said
bluntly.

The old women both looked a little shocked at my frank-
ness, but I went on boldly. "Bergit's marriage to my father
is the best thing that's ever happened to me, but somehow
I've stood between them. My father and I have never gotten along well. I could never forgive him for parting me
from my mother. But lately I have begun to feel differently.
I want a life of my own, to feel independent."

"Good for you, Merrie," said Tante Helga, "you've had a
hard struggle, but now you are talking sense. I think perhaps Onkel Lars and I may be able to help you a little to

become independent."

I wondered what she had in mind. Surely this was some-thing I must do for myself.

Presently I slipped away and went into the house. I grabbed a hunk of cheese and a couple of apples from the kitchen and stuffed them into my pockets. Then I took the path through the woods behind the house that led up the hill.

Soon the path narrowed and grew steeper, the trees thinned out, and I had to go more slowly and carefully. I picked my way upwards, climbing all the time, till I left the trees behind and emerged into a small high valley where there was a herd of goats and a little shelter. I stopped to rest for a few minutes and looking back the way I had come, I saw far below me the whole countryside spread out at the foot of the mountains, and Onkel Lars' farm with its little sloping fields. I was glad I had come so high, it gave me a new perspective. I remembered something Giller had once said to me about the mountains. "It's a wider world up there, a man can see farther."

I plodded on, and after I had been climbing for what seemed like hours, I saw ahead of me a little grass platform.

I left the path, scrambled on to the platform and was star-tled by the sound of roaring that filled the air. Beyond the edge of the platform hung a cloud of mist, of spray, and suddenly I knew where I was. I had climbed to the High Fall! Once years ago I had been there with Bergit. I remem-bered it was a terrifying place, the spray rose from an enor-mously high waterfall.

I lay down flat and began to edge myself forward till I could see the torrent of water, like a great horsetail, plung-ing down hundreds of feet to the river far below. Tiny toy cars were moving up and down the road, or were parked at the foot of the fall, and miniature people stood looking up at it. I had a feeling of omnipotence, as if I were in control of the puppet-life far below me. I wriggled a little nearer to the edge, fascinated by the huge cascade of water. The roar of it deafened my ears and lulled my senses, shutting me into the world of my own mind. I began to think about myself—and about Bergit and my father. I wondered how they would get along; would they be happy together? Would they grow close to one another again as they had been at first? Surely it would be better for them if I stayed away, perhaps for good. They'd be much happier without me.

Perhaps the time had come for me to make a break. I felt sure enough of myself to get along without them, to stand on my own feet, to make my own decisions, to rely on myself.

I wriggled a little closer to the sweep of water, how horribly easy it would be to slip down . . . over the edge!

The grass was very smooth and I had worked myself further forward than I realized . . . better move back . . . at once! I looked down over the fall, grew dizzy and lost my nerve. My limbs became paralyzed with terror. I dared not move at all! I could only dig my nails and toes into the slippery grass and hang on for dear life.

I shut my eyes, praying for the dizziness, the panic to pass. Somehow I must wriggle back to safety, but I was terrified that I would not have the strength to hold on long enough.

"Steady now," said a man's voice in Norwegian, and my ankles were grasped by two strong hands that pulled me back, back, back.

I lay on the platform of grass weak with fright, and in a cold sweat. I was shaking all over, my face hidden in my arms. Then gradually my body began to relax and I burst into tears of desperate relief.

23

I DON'T KNOW HOW LONG I LAY THERE, BUT IT CAN'T HAVE been for more than a few minutes, then a hand began to stroke my hair and the same voice said, "Come on, you're all right now. Cheer up."

I stopped crying and raised my head to peer through my hair at the man who had saved me—it was Erik Petersen!

I sat up at once, brushing my tears away and turned to him. "Erik!" I said shakily "Erik Petersen!"

"Merrie?" he cried astonished, "Merrie! It's you! I had no idea—I couldn't see your face. What on earth were you doing so near the waterfall? You gave me a fright, I can tell you. I was afraid you were going over before I could reach you. Are you all right now?"

"Yes thank you. I'm all right," I said. "But it's a good thing you came along when you did."

"How did you get into such a dangerous position?"

"I didn't notice how close I'd gotten to the edge till I tried to get back and found I couldn't move at all. I suppose I lost my nerve. Anyway thank you Erik for saving me. I'm glad it was you and not some stranger."

He patted my shoulder and looked anxiously into my face.

"Can you walk home?" he asked. "You're very pale."

"Oh yes, I'm quite all right now," I assured him.

"Come along then," he said, pulling me to my feet. "I ought to get back to work. I came up after a lost goat and her kid. Does anyone know where you are?"

I shook my head. My legs still felt very wobbly, from fright I suppose, and suddenly for no reason tears began to trickle down my cheeks again. Erik gave me his handkerchief and I mopped my eyes and blew my nose, and then, I don't quite know how it happened, but I turned to him and hid my face against his chest. His arms came around me, protective and comfortingly strong, and I clung to him, rubbing my cheek against the roughness of his shirt. It seemed the most natural thing to do, and I felt I wanted to stay like that for ever.

"Merrie," he said gently. "Merrie, you're safe now. Try to forget the fright you've had. I'm going to take you home to the farm, to Fru Helga."

He kept a supporting arm round me till I felt steadier, and where the path was steepest, he took my hand and helped me down. My knees still felt weak and I was grateful to him, he was so kind, so thoughtful. We came down slowly, and he made me stop and rest every now and then; but at last we saw the farm not far below us. To my surprise Onkel Lars and his dog were plodding up the path towards us.

"They must be anxious about you; your uncle is coming

to look for you," said Erik.

"Don't tell them, please, don't tell them how you found me," I begged, for I realized how idiotic I had been. They'd expect someone of my age to have more sense.

"All right," Erik agreed, "but you won't ever go up there alone again, will you?"

"Never," I promised. "Never again."

They were all very concerned about me at the farm when we got back.

"You're as white as a sheet, child! Whatever made you disappear without a word like that?" asked Tante Helga. "Away all day and no food—we have been really worried about you!"

"She's worn out, that's what's wrong," Tante Sophie said. "I expect she walked too far and got lost."

"I went up to the High Fall, but I didn't get lost," I stated proudly.

"The High Fall!" exclaimed the two old women. "No wonder you are tired, child. How good of you to bring her home, Erik."

"I went up there to look for a lost goat," said Erik. "I didn't find the goat—but I found Merrie! She is very tired so it took us a long time to get home."

Tante Helga pressed Erik to stay for supper, but he would not. He wanted to get back to his children.

After he had gone, I was packed off to bed and Tante Helga brought me my supper on a tray, while Tante Sophie fussed round me like an old hen, and I rather enjoyed being fussed over.

Next morning I had recovered from my adventure, and after breakfast Tante Helga called me into the kitchen. "There is something I want to say to you," she began. "On-kel Lars and I are very fond of you, Merrie. We want you to remember that there is always a home for you here with us, any time you want to come. But at your age you like to feel independent, I know, to have a corner of your own, so we have decided to give you the little grass-roofed house— 'Merrie's house' you used to call it."

"The little grass-roofed house?" I repeated. "For me? To keep? For always?"

I just couldn't believe it—it was too good to be possible, a place of my very own—it was wonderful! The new tenant for whom it had been repaired was *me*, so now it really was "Merrie's house."

"Oh, Tante Helga," I cried. "How can I ever thank you and Onkel Lars! It is the most wonderful present anyone could ever think of!"

I flung my arms round her and hugged her and my heart sang.

"Can we go and see it?" I asked. "Now, at once? I noticed the other day that it had been repaired and put in order and I meant to ask you who had come to live there, but I forgot. I never dreamed that it was ready for me."

We went out of the back door and across the field to where the little house stood, its grass roof gay with growing buttercups and a tiny birch tree.

Tante Helga took the key from the ledge over the door and let me in. Inside it was spotless. There was a table, two chairs and a couch bed with a gay homemade cover. On the shelves by the electric hot plate there were plates and cups, a coffee pot and a cooking pan. There was even a tiny bathroom, and above the bed, a bookshelf full of books. I stood enchanted, enraptured with my little kingdom, my miniature home.

"It's mine," I kept saying. "It's really mine," but I still couldn't quite believe it.

"It's got everything. I could *live* here when I'm older!" I exclaimed.

"Yes, you could, but I hope you'll sometimes stay with us," said Tante Helga laughing. I knew that she was teasing me.

"I just don't know how to thank you both," I said again. "It's about the kindest thing that's ever happened to me. Does Bergit know?"

"Of course, and she thought it was a splendid idea," Tante Helga assured me.

"I must go and find Onkel Lars at once and thank him, too," I said, and I locked the door behind us and put the key in my pocket.

To know that I had a house of my own where I could shut out the world if I wanted to, gave me a wonderful feeling of independence, of self-assurance. I began to make plans. I had brought some school work with me, and I organized it so that I spent some time every day in my own house with my books. Sometimes I just lay on my bed looking out of the door to the mountains across the fjord, thinking and scheming and trying to decide what I wanted to do with my life. My ambitions were vague. I wanted to be happy and useful but I thought I had no special talent or inclination.

Sometimes I had a group of my friends to supper in the evening, in "Merrie's house," as everyone soon called it; young people who had played with me there on my first visit to the farm, and others I had met only recently. We would listen to records or the radio, and talk and laugh, free to make our own fun and noise.

But there were still times when I was moody and disturbed, when anxieties and uncertainties broke through the surface and I felt depressed and overshadowed. Tante Helga recognized the signs. "It's all part of growing up," she said. "You may find it helps to write it all down. Try keeping a journal, it clears one's mind and gives one a sense of proportion."

I bought an exercise book, ready to start. "But where do I begin?" I asked.

"At the beginning, when you first came to England," said Tante Helga. "Write down the things that you remember."

I began with the early days in Aunt Emma's house when I first arrived in England, my feelings of isolation in a world of strangers and the terrible knowledge that I had been severed from my mother by a father who did not love me. Then I told how Giller had pulled me out of my loneliness and given me the security I needed—while he lived. And then I explained how Bergit had come into my life. Once I got started it all came out. I wrote something every day, only a few words, or an episode that stood out vividly in my mind. Gradually as I covered the years, a pattern emerged, a design of living that made sense. I began to understand the whole complex picture, and I learned a lot about myself.

A couple of weeks went past and there was no letter from Bergit or my father, but I did not worry about them as once I would have done. I had a place at the farm, with friends all round me, and my own little house to retreat to when I wanted to be alone. I felt happier than I had been for years. My work was going well for the exams ahead, my life seemed to be expanding on to a wider canvas where many people were important. Often I found myself thinking about Erik and his children, and one day an idea came to me.

"Has Erik Petersen found anyone to help with the children since Bergit left?" I asked Tante Helga. She shook her head. "Only old Margit," she answered. "Why?"

"I would like to take Bergit's place," I said. "Would you mind? Do you think Erik would let me?"

"We can find out," said Tante Helga. "We'll ask him over for supper. I think myself it's a splendid idea." She gave me a shrewd look, then nodded her head. "Yes, a splendid idea," she repeated. "You can help those children. You know what it is like to lose your mother."

24

ERIK CAME TO SUPPER THE FOLLOWING EVENING. ALL DAY I had been thinking of him, and imagining what he would say to my suggestion. I wondered if he had given me another thought since he had rescued me from the High Fall. Suddenly it had become very important to me to see Erik again, to help him if I could and to look after his children.

When it was supper time and Erik arrived, it was Tante Helga who told him what I wanted to do. I couldn't.

"It's very kind of you, Merrie," said Erik, "but . . . well . . . it's your holiday, you don't want to work?"

"But I *do*," I cried. "I'll take good care of your children, I promise you. I'm really quite responsible. I'm sixteen this month you know, and I used to look after Daisy . . . my little sister. Your children are just about her age."

"What do you think, Fru Helga? Would you allow Merrie to work for me?"

"Why, of course, if she wants to. I think it would be good for Merrie and good for the children."

"Very well then, if you'd really like to, that's settled. Thank you, Merrie, when can you start?"

"Tomorrow," I said delightedly. "I'll come at seven o'clock in the morning." Everyone is up early on a farm, and it was only ten minutes' walk to Erik's house.

"I will pay you, of course," Erik continued. "You must treat this as a real job. How much shall I give her, Fru Helga?"

"But I can't take money from you, Erik," I protested. "It wouldn't be right to take pay for something I shall enjoy doing."

Tante Helga settled the matter.

"You will earn your money Merrie, you are very conscientious. It is quite fair that Erik pay you for what you do."

"Then please arrange it between you," I said. "I don't want to be paid, but if Erik insists then I shall save it all up for my fare back to Norway next summer."

"A very good idea," cried Onkel Lars. "Make sure she earns enough, Erik!"

I was up long before seven the next morning and the fields were still wet with dew when I arrived at Erik's house.

He was there himself to welcome me, and he took me into the kitchen where the children and Margit were having their breakfast. He told them that I was coming to help in Bergit's place.

The children were glad. They already knew me, so it did not take us long to become good friends. After Erik had gone, Margit told me what to do to help, and I very quickly found out where things were kept. I washed up the breakfast things, made the children's beds and cleaned their room, washed some of their clothes and hung them out to dry and then I took some mending outside and sat down beside them. Nils made a crown of daisies and put it on my head, and little Kari climbed shyly on to my knee and put her arms round my neck. "Make a new dress for my dolly," she begged.

Erik came in for the midday meal and when that was over I took the children into the woods to play. The day passed so quickly that it was six o'clock and time for me to go home before I knew it. My first working day was over.

"You'll come again tomorrow, won't you? *Promise*," Nils said when I left them and little Kari stretched up her arms to say goodbye.

"Yes, I'll come again tomorrow morning, I promise," I said gaily.

I was quite tired when I got back to Tante Helga, but I had had a happy day. I liked being useful. By the end of the first week, I felt I had become one of the family. Old Margit depended on me to relieve her of some of the lighter work in the house, and the children were happy to be with me wherever I was. I loved them both from the start, especially Kari whose loving ways reminded me of Daisy. She and Nils helped to fill the gap in my life that Daisy had left. It was not until I met Erik's children that I knew how much I still missed my little sister.

At first I seldom saw Erik alone, and I was quite glad. I had not met any young men, only Jim Holt, Gossie's brother, and he was so busy on the farm he had no time for girls. So it was natural that I should feel shy of Erik, especially when I remembered how I had thrown myself into his arms that day at the High Fall.

Gradually we got to know one another better as we met daily at his farm. We shared his children, and in loving them we drew closer together. He began to notice me, *really* notice me; often I saw him watching me with an expression on his face that made me very happy. I saw that he admired and liked me.

Once when the weather broke and curtains of rain hid the fjord and the mountains, I invited Nils and Kari to come to tea in my little house. We tramped along the path through the fields under a huge umbrella, squelching our way through the puddles. The children were thrilled with "Merrie's house." When it was time for tea and I set out the sandwiches and little cakes I had made early that morning, the children were more delighted than ever. "You are clever, Merrie," said Nils. "Your cakes are much better than the ones Margit makes—may I have another?"

The tea party was in full swing when Erik came striding through the rain and knocked on the door.

He shook himself like a dog as I jumped up to welcome him.

"It's so wet I knocked off work early," he said. "I thought I'd take the children home by car; I've left it on the road."

I poured him a cup of coffee, and he ate three of the little cakes I had made. I was overjoyed to have him in my own little house. It was the first time he had come there. Our usual roles were reversed, for now he was the visitor and I the host.

When tea was finished Erik said it was time to take the children home, but Nils and Kari begged for one more game.

"Let's pretend that this is our home. You are the father, Merrie is the mother, and we are the children," he said to Erik.

Erik laughed and would not be persuaded to stay; but I did not find it funny, it was an idea that appealed to me very much indeed.

When they had gone I thought about Erik for a long time, what he had said, how he had looked. I relived the time we had spent together, and wished I were older.

Later, I went to help Tante Helga get supper ready. I must have been rather quiet for she asked me if there was anything wrong. I shook my head. I could not tell her of the dreams I had had.

"At what age do Norwegian girls marry?" I asked her instead.

"That depends," she said smiling. "I was only seventeen when I married Lars, and he was nineteen, but we waited a long time for Bergit. Young people in the country marry younger than those in the towns. Why do you ask?"

"Because I want to learn everything I can about Norway so that I shall feel I *belong* here," I said.

"What are you going to be when you are grown up?" Tante Helga asked.

"A mother," I answered promptly, "and perhaps I shall be a farmer's wife like you." She thought that I was teasing her, joking.

"I mean what *work* do you want to do?" she said laughing.

"I'm not sure—something to do with children," I replied, "a children's officer, a social worker, perhaps even a teacher. I don't know yet."

"Working with children is the best kind of job, the most worthwhile work of all. You will be working for the future, Merrie. Children like you and trust you, so you will do very well," said Tante Helga. "Now go and call Onkel Lars for supper. I've made his favorite dish tonight."

Erik had told me that his younger brother Anders was coming home to the farm soon, and a day or two later he arrived from Oslo. Anders was now seventeen, not so handsome as Erik, but he had a cheerful grin and made everyone laugh. When he was around, we were all more gay, even old Margit.

Anders did not seem to remember me very well, and at first he was tongue-tied and shy with me. Then he asked me to go to a dance with him in one of the villages down the fjord, and I said I'd go. And one Sunday he took me on an expedition with some of his friends to the glacier at the end of the fjord. I had never seen a glacier, and I was thrilled to go. There were five of us, two girls and three boys, one of whom had borrowed his father's car.

We soon left the road for a rough mountain track and climbed up through a narrow valley, very desolate and bare and almost filled by a torrent of tumbling water coming from the glacier. When the track came to an end, we walked up a rocky path between huge boulders—and there it was ahead of us, a towering mass of shining ice like a giant waterfall, glistening green in the sun, with purple crevasses and shadows.

It was breathtakingly beautiful, with a majesty, a white shining glory all its own, so that I felt shaken and awed before it, as if I were standing on holy ground.

Suddenly with a loud crack like the report of a gun, a great splinter of ice broke off and cascaded down like a miniature avalanche, its roar echoing round the mountains. I jumped with fright at the unexpected noise in so silent a place, and turned and clung to Anders as once I had turned to Erik. Erik had known how to comfort and reassure me without embarrassment, but Anders was only a boy and did not know. First he laughed at my fears, teasing me for being so nervous, then he trod hard on my toe and was terribly embarrassed at his own clumsiness. His awkwardness was somehow endearing, and I felt a sudden sympathy for him, he was so young, and as untried and unsure as I was myself.

Together we ran down to the car where the others were waiting for us.

Down the valley we stopped for a picnic lunch, and a swim in the fjord before we started for home. Anders came back with me for supper at the farm—it had been a wonderful day, and I was glad I had gone with him.

That day was the beginning of a real friendship between Anders and me. He was a little ahead of me, he had just finished school and was about to start his university course. He wanted to take a science degree, but he didn't know what he wanted to do with it. We were both trying to establish ourselves, to find a place to stand. We were busy discovering, experimenting, searching; our lives spread out before us to do with them what we could. It was exciting to explore one another's thoughts and feelings, to discuss our troubles, to confess our hopes and fears, to tease and laugh together, and sometimes to quarrel. We understood one another, we were like travellers on the same train, speaking the same language. It was marvellous to know someone like Anders, I could be completely myself with him. I did not have to live up to him, to put on an act, and he accepted me just as I was. It was an easy casual relationship, undemanding and companionable. But, I gradually came to see, I did not feel for him as I did for Erik. Erik was something more.

25

THE SUMMER WAS NEARLY OVER, THE EVENINGS WERE DRAW-
ing in, and Tante Sophie had gone home. The birches
changed into their September gold, even the tiny one that
grew on the grass roof of my house. I had been so very
engrossed with the children, with Erik and Anders, with
Tante Helga and Onkel Lars, my life in Norway had become so important to me, that it was quite a shock to dis-
cover that the holiday was almost finished. In another week
or two I would have to go back to school. I did not want to
go back to England. I felt that Norway was my adopted
country, the country I would choose to live in—Erik was
here, and Anders, my friend. Of course I had not forgotten
Bergit, nor Gossie and Mrs. Holt, and Boris would be waiting for me at home. But Erik had become the center of my
life, his children and his home my chief concern. I had
found what I needed, and what it meant to be needed. I

had learned to give, not only to take. And while I had been at Onkel Lars' farm I had learned something about how to lead my own life.

I no longer felt dependent on Bergit and my father. I did not want to go back to live in Bergit's house except for holidays. I knew I would rather spend my last year at school as a boarder. Bergit and my father should be left on their own.

A letter from Bergit arrived at last, and I tore it open without my old misgivings.

It was a happy letter, everything was going well. My father was to be at the London office, no more travelling for some time.

"School starts on September 24th," Bergit wrote. "When are you coming home?" She went on to say that my exam results had arrived and I had passed three "O" levels. "Cheers!" I said aloud. "I'll get the rest next summer, and then—!"

There was a short enclosure from my father congratulating me on my exam results. He was pleased I had done well.

I folded the letters and put them in my pocket and went to find Tante Helga.

She was in the kitchen among her pots and pans. She, too, had had a letter from Bergit.

"Isn't it lovely that everything is all right again," I cried. "I'm so glad, and Bergit sounds like her old self."

Tante Helga sat down by the table, her kind face relaxed and calm.

"They're all right," she said. "Bergit and your father are making a new start. I think all will go well with them now, but what about you, Merrie? You'll be leaving us very soon. Onkel Lars and I will miss you, but I hope it will be easier for you now—for all of you at home."

"Tante Helga, I want to come back to make my home in

Norway," I said. "I love your country. I like the way people live here. I want to be one of them. I have another year at school, but after that I want to come back here. Bergit and my father will get on better without me. Perhaps they will have other children, I hope they do." I spoke with confidence. I knew what I wanted.

"It all sounds quite sensible," Tante Helga commented, "but what will your father have to say? He'll want you to go to a university or take a training in England."

"I don't think he'll try to stop me from coming over here. It would be a good solution," I said. "And I can take a training in Oslo as well as I can in England, can't I?"

"Yes, I expect you can, but you'll have to see what your father and Bergit say about it," said Tante Helga. "Of course there are the holidays. You could spend the summers over here, your little house will always be ready for you, and a warm welcome from us."

"I know, dear Tante, and I am so grateful," I said. "But holidays are not enough, I want to *live* over here, to settle— perhaps to marry a Norwegian." Tante Helga chuckled.

"Oh, so that's it!" she said. "Well, you could do a lot worse. You're both very young, but you've plenty of time, and he's a good boy. There's no hurry, you can wait for a few years till he is qualified—if you don't change your minds!"

I laughed happily. She was thinking of Anders of course, but Erik was the one I had set my heart on. I did not think I would ever change my mind about *him*.

On my last day at the farm, I felt very close to Tante Helga and Onkel Lars. They had been so wonderfully good to me I wanted to thank them, but I could not find the right words!

I thought of all the others who had helped me along—

Giller, Aunt Emma, Mrs. Holt and Gossie, Miss Chiswick, and most of all Bergit. It was thanks to all of them that I had been able to find a place of my own in the world.

On my last evening Tante Helga invited Erik and his children, and Anders and old Margit to come to supper. It was a special treat for the children, who were allowed to stay up late.

We were a gay party, and when Onkel Lars got out his violin and started to play, even old Margit's toes began to dance.

Afterwards I walked back part of the way with them across the fields. Anders carried Kari on his back, and Nils hung on to his father's hand. I desperately wanted a few minutes alone with Erik to say goodbye to him, but I did not know how to manage it.

But when we had nearly reached his farm, he sent the others on ahead. "Help to get the children off to bed, Anders," he said. "I'll take Merrie back to Fru Helga's."

I hugged the children, who did not want to say goodbye. "You'll come back again?" they insisted, "promise you'll come back again!"

"Of course I will!" I promised.

"Goodbye, Merrie—see you," said Anders in his casual way. "I might even write to you. Take care of yourself till next summer."

"Goodbye—goodbye," they called as Erik and I walked back together, hand in hand through the dusky fields till we came to my little house.

I turned to him then—and suddenly I was in his arms, and my arms went round his neck.

"Erik—Erik—I can't bear to leave you," I whispered, "I don't want to go home. This is where I belong. Everything I love best is here with you. I want to come back again next summer—and stay for always."

"It's a long time till next summer," Erik said gently. "You may change your mind. You're still very young."

"I'll never change my mind about you," I vowed. "It has nothing to do with age. I promise I'll come back next summer if you want me to."

His arms tightened round me, and he laid his cheek against the top of my head. I felt myself relaxing, expanding, sprouting like a spindly thorn tree brought out into the sunshine, leaves uncurling, buds unfolding, hiding the thorns in a burst of miraculous blossom.

"I'll wait for you," he promised. "I'll wait for you to grow up, my little dark flower."

26

Back in England, I was surprised to find how good it was to be home again.

I found I was looking at everything with new eyes. I had a purpose in life, a direction, and I meant to get on with it.

But it did not all work out quite as I had planned.

Only a few days after I got back my father became seriously ill and had to go into the hospital with some bug he must have picked up on his travels. So I couldn't be a boarder at school that first term. I wanted to live at home to keep Bergit company, and then after my father came out of the hospital, she needed my help during his convalescence. Everything was on such a different and better footing that I enjoyed being at home. I was glad I could be useful and I gave all the help I could, gladly. My father had changed a lot, he was much less nervous and irritable and seemed somehow more complete, as if he had found an inner tranquility, a lasting peace of mind. But physically he was very weak and dependent on Bergit, and I tried to relieve her as much as possible and to give her some rest.

He and I were alone enough for us to get used to one another, to get to know one another on a different level. I lost my nervousness with him and began to talk to him as a friend. It was he who persuaded me to follow Miss Chiswick's advice and to finish my education in England.

"You can spend your summers in Norway if you want to," he said. "I suppose there is a boy friend out there?" I smiled at the idea of calling Erik a "boy friend"—he was so much more.

Early in the term Miss Chiswick had talked seriously to me about my work at school, which she said was well above average. I told her my ideas of what I wanted to be. I also told her that I wanted to get married when I was old enough.

She urged me to try to go to a university, and because I liked and admired her and had a great respect for her judgment, I decided to follow her advice.

"Don't waste your time pottering around waiting to get married," she said. "Get on with a career of your own. You'll make a better wife in the end."

I told Bergit about Erik, of course. "You're too young for him now," she said, "but in three or four years the gap between you will have narrowed and you'll be on a more equal footing. You can give a lot to him and to the children, but don't be in too much of a hurry, darling. Give yourself a chance to grow up first, and to have some fun."

"You don't think I'm just a romantic school girl dreaming about a man who is too old for me?" I asked.

"Certainly not—when you are twenty he won't be too old for you. And I have a feeling you won't change your mind about Erik. Knowing you both, I think you are very well suited to one another. But what does Erik think?" "I'm not quite certain yet," I confessed. "He says he's waiting for me to grow up." "Well I don't see why you and Erik shouldn't be extremely happy living on his farm," Bergit continued. "He is a very intelligent young man and interested in lots of things besides farming. It isn't as it was in the old days when my father was young. That area really was isolated then. There was no road from the town, and the only way to reach the farms and villages was by boat on the fjord. Then they really *were* cut off, and life must have been hard and very quiet, especially in the winter. Now with proper communications, and radio and a good road, things are much more lively. You'll always find plenty to do, and I don't think you'll ever feel bored for long."

I was grateful to Bergit for being on our side, for giving me new hope and encouragement for the future.

As soon as I had arrived home from Norway I had begun watching for an opportunity to give the little jade back to my father. Once he was out of hospital and beginning to feel better I waited for the right moment.

It came on a Sunday morning when Bergit was sleeping late. I took my father's breakfast into his room, then I went and fetched the little jade. I held it out to him and sat down on his bed. I told him how I had stolen it and all that had happened afterwards.

After the first shock of finding that it was safe, my father listened quietly without interrupting me and without any signs of anger.

"You have been robbing yourself," he said when I had finished. "Your mother gave the jade to me for safe keeping for *you*. It's a long story but I'll try to tell you.

"When my job ended in Malaya and I decided to come home, it was a bad time out there. The 'Emergency' as it was called, had started. You must remember yourself the trouble with the Communists—raids, ambushes, shootings, burnings, had all begun in parts of the country, and our rubber estate was already on the fringes of it.

"Nowhere was safe, no one knew what might happen. Your mother was afraid for your life. She wanted me to take you home to England with me, to bring you up here," my father explained. "It was very hard for her to let you go.

"Merrie—I was very fond of your mother, but I did not want her for my wife. I did not want to marry her, it would have been impossible. She was a simple village girl. She'd have hated England and English ways. She knew this as well as I did, but you were the difficulty. She wanted me to bring you to England with me, to bring you up here, to give you a better chance in life than she had had. And Aunt Emma wanted it, too. But your mother had great pride, she wanted to have a share in helping you to make your way to a better life, she wanted to provide you with the means to be independent. Her whole family supported her in this. They presented me with the little jade, their family treasure, to keep for you, your 'dowry' they called it. I did not want to take it, it was very precious to them, but they made me. That's how it came to England."

I was touched and very proud that so poor a family had shown such pride in me, had cared so much about me.

"What has happened to my mother?" I asked. "Have you never tried to find out?"

"Never until my last trip abroad. Then I had a few days in Singapore and I made some inquiries," said my father. "Your mother is dead. She was killed in a Communist ambush only a few weeks after we left for England."

I nodded my head. I did not know what to say. I could not feel the loss of a mother I had not seen since I was six years old, yet her death made me sad.

"What do *you* feel about it?" I asked my father.

"Her death is a kind of release for me," he said. "As long as I thought she lived, I felt guilty about her. I wish I had had the courage to find out about her long ago. I thought I could forget her, but I never have. You are very like her, Merrie."

"What happens to the little jade now?" I asked, picking it up and holding it against my cheek.

"We must find out what it is worth and insure it," said my father. "We ought to know its money value."

"I shall never sell it unless I have to," I cried, "but perhaps it should be used for sending me to a university? Isn't that what my mother wanted?"

"Oh, there's no need for that," said my father smiling. "I can provide you with enough cash, especially if you receive a grant. The little jade must be kept as an heirloom."

"Then you must keep it for me till I marry," I said. "I'd like to have it in my own home some day. I'd like my children to grow up with it, to know what it has meant to me, and how it came to belong to me."

Some day, when I am older, I will go back to Norway, not just for the summer holidays but to live there, and to work among the people I love, some day when Erik and I are married—some day.